D0403182

VOICES
FROM
FRANCE

Selected and Translated by Miriam Morton

FIERCE AND GENTLE WARRIORS
Stories by Mikhail Sholokhov

THE FIRST SONG
by Semyon Rosenfeld

THE HOUSE OF THE FOUR WINDS
by Colette Vivier

SHADOWS AND LIGHT
Stories by Anton Chekhov

VOICES FROM FRANCE
Ten stories by
French Nobel prize winners

VOICES FROM FROM FRANCE

TEN STORIES BY FRENCH NOBEL PRIZE WINNERS

SELECTED AND EDITED
BY MIRIAM MORTON

DOUBLEDAY & COMPANY, INC.
GARDEN CITY, NEW YORK

1513010

For Alice
M.M.

ACKNOWLEDGMENTS

The translation of the story "L'Hôte" (The Guest) by Albert Camus appears with the permission of Alfred A. Knopf, Inc., publishers of the volume *Exile and the Kingdom.*

The translation of the stories "Crainquebille" and "Putois" by Anatole France are included with the permission of Calmann-Lévy, Éditeur.

The translation of the excerpt from *Pierre et Luce* (Pierre and Luce) by Romain Rolland is included with the permission of Éditions Albin Michel.

The translation of "Le Retour de L'Enfant Prodigue" (The Return of the Prodigal Son) is included with the permission of Éditions Gallimard.

The translation of the excerpt "Le Pénitencier" (The Reformatory) from the novel *Les Thibault* (The World of the Thibaults) by Roger Martin du Gard appears with the permission of Éditions Gallimard.

The translation of the story "Conte de Noël" (A Christmas Tale) by François Mauriac is included with the permission of Éditions Bernard Grasset.

The translation by Lloyd Alexander of the story "Le Mur" (The Wall) by Jean-Paul Sartre appears with the permission of New Directions Publishers and Mr. Alexander.

CONTENTS

(Miriam Morton translated all of the following stories, except Jean-Paul Sartre's "The Wall," which was translated by Lloyd Alexander.)

INTRODUCTION

The eight short stories and the two self-contained excerpts from novels which comprise this book are drawn from the writings of an almost equal number of illustrious French authors of our century. Each of these eight writers was awarded the Nobel Prize for Literature. France, with twelve such awards, has received more than any other country. The work of all of her Nobel writers of creative *prose,* from the folklorist (as well as major poet) Frédéric Mistral to the existentialist author Jean-Paul Sartre, is represented in this volume. The Nobel laureates omitted are: the poets Sully-Prudhomme and St.-John Perse, the Belgian dramatist Maurice Maeterlinck, who spent most of his life in France and was therefore given the award as a French writer, and the philosopher Henri Bergson.

Apart from the obvious advantage of having so lavish a literary feast inside the covers of a single book, the sum of the selections offers a good glimpse into the brilliance, vitality, and diversity of French literature. It serves to initiate the

young-adult reader into French letters and to give him a
foretaste of the rich reading experience in store for him
when he later goes on to the longer works by the same authors.
The stories also reveal in a significant way how these authors
reflect the concerns, the values, and the highest hopes of
their own generations. It may be said that their ideas of their
chosen art and of the writer's role are faithfully represented
in the words of Albert Camus in his acceptance speech of
the Nobel award:

> I cannot live as a person without my art. And yet I have
> never set that art above everything else. It is essential to me,
> on the contrary, because it excludes no one and allows me to
> live, just as I am, on a footing with all. To me art is not a
> solitary delight. It is a means of stirring the greatest number
> of men by providing them with a privileged image of our
> common joys and woes. Hence it forces the artist not to
> isolate himself; it subjects him to the humblest and most
> universal truth. . . . The artist fashions himself in that
> ceaseless oscillation from himself to others, midway between
> the beauty he cannot do without and the community from
> which he cannot tear himself. This is why true artists scorn
> nothing. . . . The true artist accepts as completely as pos-
> sible the two trusts that constitute the nobility of his calling:
> the service of truth and the service of freedom.*

The stories in this volume intrigue the modern mind, for
they mirror present-day realities. They evoke compassion and
wonder, and occasionally laughter, at the contradictions, the
ironies, the absurdities, and the neuroticism universally common to the human condition. In other words, they have vital
relevance today. And it is this relevance and modernity,
together with their dramatic force and energy of thought, that
animate these stories and render them absorbing and enjoyable
for the contemporary reader, both the young-adult reader and
the more seasoned one. In fact, one finds an astounding con-
temporaneity among all the world's great writers.

* Translated by Justin O'Brien

Without wishing to impose my own responses on the reader, I have supplied a brief commentary on each author and on the selection from his works. The object of the commentaries is to give the reader some essential background information and a clue here and there which might deepen his insight into the core of the story's theme, or the author's ideas on the theme, or the inner drama of the characters. The reader is certainly invited to proceed as independently as he wishes, respecting his own reactions.

In doing the translating, I followed the original text with respectful fidelity, resisting the temptation to improvise. Nevertheless, some of the most subtle elements of style might have been lost. I fully agree with the translator who said that "words are very patriotic," for they so often resist complete assimilation into another language.

I did not, in any sense, adapt any of the stories. Just a few words in only two of the selections have been omitted. This was done, with reluctance, to avoid unwieldly footnotes in one case and possible embarrassment in the other. The few omitted words are not, in my judgment, particularly significant to the stories.

In arranging the sequence of the selections, I did not follow a chronological or alphabetical order. I arranged the stories in such a way as to highlight their diversity, in order to afford the reader greater pleasure.

Miriam Morton

THE GUEST

Albert Camus

ALBERT CAMUS is the most widely read French author in America. Translations of nearly all of his essays, novels, plays, and short stories have been published in the United States. Camus was born in 1913, in Algeria, into utter material and cultural poverty. Surmounting destitution and early tuberculosis, he acquired a good education. He began to be published at the age of twenty-four, and his famous novel, *The Stranger,* already a modern classic, appeared only two years later. Since his untimely death in 1960, in a highway accident, his popularity in America has, in fact, grown. For his was a passionate voice in the wasteland and bewilderment of our age.

Camus appeals particularly to young people who, like him, seek values to live by and answers to questions touching on the meaning of life *on earth* and the destiny of mankind in the nuclear age. They love and respect him because of his uninhibited idealism and the creative inspiration with which he affirms his moral convictions.

The citation to Albert Camus on his receiving the Nobel award (in 1957) reads:

> For his important literary production, which with clear-sighted earnestness illuminates the problems of the human conscience of our time.

"The Guest," is one of six stories comprising *Exile and the Kingdom,* among Camus' last works, published in 1957. The title of the volume expresses the author's essential view of the man of integrity, who "exiles" himself from the world whose moral shoddiness he cannot accept and lives in his inner "kingdom" in which his spirit may be restored. The French schoolteacher in "The Guest" is an exile in such a kingdom. The *absurd,* an essential element of human life, thwarts his motives regarding his "guest," the Arab prisoner.

The arid plateau, the unseasonal blizzard followed by the consuming sun, create nature's backdrop for the inner drama of the characters.

The spareness of language with which Camus achieves the impact of his story is typical of his style of writing, which, in turn, stems from his way of looking at things with clear-sightedness, directness, and honesty.

As in many of his writings, Camus portrays in this story the pathos and the nobility to be found in the humblest lives.

THE GUEST

The schoolteacher watched the two men climb toward his
place. One was on horseback, the other on foot. They hadn't
yet reached the steep grade leading to his hillside school.
They were making slow progress in the snow and over the
stones of the immense stretch of high, desolate plateau.
From time to time the horse stumbled. Its hoofs couldn't
yet be heard where the schoolteacher was standing, but he
could see the steamy breath coming from its nostrils. At
least one of the men knew the region. They were following
the trail that had disappeared several days before under the
dirty white blanket of snow. The schoolteacher calculated
that they would not reach the top of the hill for another half
hour. It was cold. He went into the schoolhouse to get his
sweater.

He crossed the empty, frigid schoolroom. On the blackboard, the four rivers of France, traced with chalk of four
different colors, had been flowing toward their estuaries for
the past three days. Heavy snows had come in mid-October

after eight months of drought, and without the transition of rain, and his twenty or so pupils, who lived in the villages scattered over the plateau, had been staying home. They had to wait for better weather. Daru now heated only the single room that constituted his lodging. It adjoined the classroom and also gave onto the plateau, to the east. One of his windows, like the classroom's, opened to the south. On that side, the schoolhouse was only a few kilometers from where the plateau began to slope toward the south. In clear weather you could see the violet mass of the mountain range with its opening to the desert.

Feeling a little warmer, Daru returned to the window from which he had first noticed the two men. He could no longer see them. This meant that they had begun to come up the steep rise. The sky was less overcast; the snow had stopped falling during the night. The morning had risen with a murky light that scarcely grew brighter as the clouds lifted. Now, at two in the afternoon, it seemed as if the day were just beginning. Yet this was better than the three previous days, when the heavy snow was falling in unrelieved darkness and the shifting winds rattled the double door of the classroom. Daru had then waited out the storm, spending long hours in his room and leaving it only to go down into the lean-to in order to feed the chickens and get some coal. Fortunately, the delivery truck from Tadjid, the nearest village to the north, had brought his supplies two days before the tempest. The truck would return in forty-eight hours.

Actually he had enough to sit out a siege. His small room was cluttered with bags of wheat which the authorities had left with him for distribution to those of his pupils whose families were victims of the drought. Misfortune had struck all the families, since they were all poor. Daru planned to give out a daily ration to the children. He knew that they had gone without food during these bad days. Perhaps one of the fathers or one of the big brothers would come before

dark and he could let them have the wheat. They simply had
to be carried over to the next harvest. There was no alterna-
tive. Shiploads of wheat were now arriving from France, and
the worst was over. But it would be hard to forget that
famine, those ragged ghosts drifting in the sunlight, the
plateau burned month after month, the earth literally scorched
and gradually shriveling up, every stone splintering into dust
underfoot. The sheep had died then by the thousands; also
a few men here and there, sometimes without anyone's knowing.

Witnessing such poverty, this man who lived like a monk
in his remote schoolhouse, content with the little he had and
with his rugged life, had felt like a lord with his whitewashed
walls, narrow cot, crude bookshelves, his well, and his modest
weekly supply of food and water. Then suddenly the snow,
without warning, without the relief of rain. The region was
like that, cruel to live in even had it not been for its people,
who did not make things easier either. But Daru was born
here. Anywhere else he felt like an exile.

He went outside and crossed the terrace. The two men were
now halfway up the slope. He recognized the one on horseback—it was Balducci, an old gendarme. Daru had known
him for a long time. Balducci was leading an Arab at the
end of a rope. The man was walking behind him, his hands
tied and his head bowed. The gendarme waved a greeting to
which Daru didn't respond, totally absorbed as he was in
looking at the Arab. The prisoner was dressed in a loose,
faded overgarment called a *djellabah;* he had sandals on his
feet but he also wore heavy, raw-wool socks; his head was
covered with a *chèche,* a narrow, short scarf twisted into a tur-
ban. The two men were approaching. Balducci had reined
in his animal so as not to pull too hard on the rope, thus
avoiding hurting the Arab. The group was advancing slowly.

When they were within earshot, Balducci shouted, "Did

the three kilometers from El Ameur in one hour!" Daru
didn't answer. He stood there, short and square in his thick
sweater, and watched them climb. Not once did the Arab
raise his head.

"Hello," said Daru when they reached the terrace. "Come
in and warm up." Balducci dismounted with difficulty; he
didn't let go of the rope. He smiled at the schoolteacher from
under his bristling mustache. His small dark eyes, deep-set
under his tanned forehead, and his mouth surrounded by
wrinkles, made him look stern and determined. Daru took
the bridle, led the horse to the shed, and returned to the two
men who were now waiting for him in the schoolhouse. He
took them to his room. "I'm going to heat the classroom,"
he said. "We'll be more comfortable there."

When he entered his room again, Balducci was on the
couch. He had undone the rope which had tied him to the
Arab. The Arab was now squatting near the stove. His hands
still bound, the *chèche* pushed back on his head, he was looking in the direction of the window. Daru noticed at first only
his enormous lips, full, smooth, almost Negroid. He noticed
that his nose was thin. His eyes were black and feverish.
The raised *chèche* uncovered a stubborn brow, and the
man's whole face, weathered and somewhat discolored with
the cold, had an anxious and rebellious look, which struck
Daru when the Arab, turning his face toward him, looked
him straight in the eyes. "Go into the other room," the
schoolteacher said. "I'll make you some mint tea."

"Thanks," said Balducci. "What a job I've got! Can't wait
to retire." And addressing his prisoner in Arabic: "Come
along, you." The Arab got up and, holding his tied-up
wrists in front of him, slowly walked to the classroom.

With the tea Daru brought a chair. But Balducci had en-
throned himself in the front on a pupil's table, and the
Arab was squatting against the teacher's platform facing the
stove, which was between the desk and the window. Offering

the glass of tea to the prisoner, Daru hesitated when he saw
his bound hands. "Could you perhaps untie him?"

"Sure," said Balducci. "That was only for the trip." And
he started to get to his feet. But Daru placed the glass on the
floor and knelt down beside the Arab; without saying anything the Arab watched him with his feverish eyes as he un-
tied his hands. He rubbed his freed swollen wrists against
each other, lifted the glass of tea, and drank the scalding
liquid in eager little sips.

"Well," said Daru to the gendarme, "where will you be going now?"

Balducci withdrew his mustache from the tea. "We stay
here, son."

"Odd schoolchildren! Are you staying the night?"

"No. I'm going back to El Ameur. And you will hand over
this fellow at Tinguit. The police there know he's on his
way."

Balducci looked at Daru with a friendly little smile.

"What kind of story is this?" said the schoolteacher. "Are
you pulling my leg?"

"No, son. Those are the orders."

"Orders? But I'm not . . ." Daru hesitated; he didn't
want to offend the old Corsican. "I mean, that's not my occupation."

"How's that? . . . You know that doesn't mean anything
nowadays. In wartime people are called upon to do all kinds
of jobs."

"Then I'll wait for a declaration of war."

Balducci nodded.

"All right. But these are the orders and they concern you
too. It appears that things are brewing. There's talk of a coming revolt. We are, so to speak, mobilized."

Daru continued to look determined.

"Listen, son," said Balducci, "I like you a lot, you must
know that. There are only about a dozen of us in El Ameur

to patrol the territory of the entire department—that's not many, small though the department is, and I have to get back there. They told me to hand this 'zebra' over to you and return in a hurry. Back there he couldn't be guarded safely. His village was up in arms, they wanted to get him out. So you must take him to Tinguit. Do it in the daytime. It's only about twenty kilometers from here; that shouldn't strain a vigorous fellow like you. After that you can forget the whole thing. You can then come back to your kids and to your serene life."

They heard the horse snorting and stamping the ground on the other side of the wall. Daru looked out the window. The weather was certainly clearing, and it was lighter now over the snow-covered plateau. When all the snow had melted, the sun would dominate again and scorch the fields of stone once more. For days the unchanging sky would keep shedding its dry light over the desolate expanse, where there was nothing to suggest the existence of man.

Turning to Balducci, Daru said, "But tell me, what has he done?" And before the gendarme opened his mouth to answer, he asked, "Does he speak French?"

"A little. We looked for him for a month, but they were hiding him. He killed his cousin."

"Is he against us?"

"I don't think so. But you can't be sure."

"Why did he kill him?"

"A family squabble, I think. It seemed one owed some grain to the other. It's not clear. In short, he killed his cousin with a blow of the billhook. You know, like a sheep, *zic!*"

Balducci made the gesture of striking with a blade across his throat, and the Arab, his attention attracted, looked at him uneasily. Daru felt a sudden wrath against this man, against all men and their sordid malice, their endless hatreds, their lust for blood.

But the kettle was purring on the stove. He served Balducci

more tea, hesitated, then served the Arab a second time; again the prisoner drank avidly. His raised arms drew the *djellabah* half open, and the schoolteacher noticed his chest, thin and muscular.

"Thanks, son," Balducci said. "And now I'm off."

He got up and went over to the Arab, taking a small rope from his pocket.

"What are you doing?" Daru asked bluntly.

Balducci, nonplused, showed him the rope.

"You don't need to do it."

The old gendarme hesitated.

"All right, have it your way. I suppose you're armed?"

"I have my hunting gun."

"Where?"

"In my trunk."

"You ought to keep it near your bed."

"Why? I have nothing to fear."

"You're mad, son! If they stage a rebellion, no one will be safe—we'll all be in the same boat."

"I'll defend myself. I'll have time to see them coming."

Balducci began to laugh, then suddenly the mustache again covered his white teeth.

"You'll have time, you say? Fine. And I say you have always been a little cracked. But that's why I like you; my son was like that."

At the same time he pulled out his revolver and placed it on the desk.

"Keep it, I don't need two weapons from here to El Ameur."

The revolver sparkled against the black paint of the table. When the gendarme turned toward him, the schoolteacher smelled the odor of leather and horses.

"Listen, Balducci," Daru said suddenly, "all this disgusts me, and worst of all this specimen of yours. But I won't hand him over. I'll fight, yes, if it's necessary. But not that."

The old gendarme stood in front of him and looked at him severely.

"You are acting like a fool," he said slowly. "I don't like it either. You don't get used to putting a rope on a man, even after years of doing it, and you're even, yes, ashamed. But you can't let them do as they please."

"I won't hand him over," Daru repeated.

"It's an order, son, and I'm telling you this again."

"I understand. Repeat to them what I've said to you: I won't hand him over."

Balducci made an apparent effort to weigh the matter. He looked at the Arab and at Daru. At last he came to a decision.

"No, I won't tell them anything. If you want to stand against us, do as you please; I'll not denounce you. I have an order to deliver the prisoner; I'm doing so. Now you'll sign this paper for me."

"There's no need to do that. I'll not deny that you left him with me."

"Don't be difficult with me. I know you'll tell the truth. You are known here, and you are a man. But you must sign, that's the rule."

Daru opened his drawer, took out a small, square bottle of purple ink, the red wooden penholder with the "sergeant-major" penpoint that he used for tracing models of penmanship, and he signed. The gendarme folded the paper carefully and put it into his billfold. Then he moved toward the door.

"I'll see you off," Daru said.

"No," said Balducci. "It's no use being polite. You have offended me."

He looked at the Arab, motionless in the same spot, sniffed with vexation, and turned away toward the door. "Good-by, son," he said. The door slammed behind him. Balducci suddenly loomed outside the window and then disappeared. His footsteps were muffled by the snow. The horse stirred on the other side of the wall and the chickens fluttered in fright. A moment later Balducci passed again in front of the window, pulling the horse by the bridle. He walked toward the slope without turning around and disappeared from sight with the horse following him. A large stone could be heard softly bouncing down.

Daru returned to the prisoner, who hadn't stirred, never taking his eyes off him. "Wait," the schoolteacher said in Arabic and went toward the adjoining room. As he was crossing the threshold, he thought of something, went to the desk, picked up the revolver and stuck it in his pocket. Then, without looking back, he went into his room.

For some time he remained stretched out on his couch, watching the sky gradually close in, and listening to the silence. It was this silence that had disturbed him during the first days here, after the war. He had asked for a position in the little town at the bottom of the foothills that separate the desert from the high plateau. It is there that the rock walls, green and black to the north, pink and lavender to the south, mark the frontier of eternal summer. He had instead been given a position farther north, on the plateau itself. At first the solitude and the stillness had been hard for him on this barren land inhabited only by stones. Here and there furrows suggested cultivation, but they had been dug only to locate a certain kind of stone good for construction. People plowed here only to harvest rocks. Occasionally the thin soil blown into the hollows would be scraped up to enrich the earth of meager village gardens. But that was all—nothing but stones covering three quarters of the region. Towns sprang up here, flourished, then disappeared; men passed through, loved one another or were at each other's throats, then died. In this desolation, neither he nor his guest mattered. And yet, Daru knew that outside this desert neither he nor the other could really have lived.

He got up. No noise came from the classroom. He was amazed at the frank joy that came over him at the mere thought that the Arab might have fled and that he would be alone again, with no decision to make. But the prisoner was there. He had merely stretched out between the stove and the desk. His eyes were open, and he was staring at the ceiling. In this position, his thick lips were particularly noticeable; they gave him a sullen look.

"Come," Daru said. The Arab got up and followed him. In his room the schoolteacher pointed to a chair near the table at the window. The Arab sat down without taking his eyes off Daru.

"Are you hungry?"

"Yes," the prisoner said.

Daru set two places. He took flour and oil, kneaded a flat cake in a plate, and lighted the butane stove. While the cake was frying, he went to the shed for some cheese, eggs, dates, and condensed milk. When the cake was done, he put it on the windowsill to cool, heated some condensed milk diluted with water and, lastly, began to beat up the eggs for an omelette. His arm brushed against the revolver stuck in his right pocket. He put the bowl down, went into the classroom, and put the revolver in his desk drawer. He came back to the room. Night was falling. He turned on the light, and served the Arab. "Eat," he said. The Arab broke off a piece of the flat cake, lifted it avidly to his mouth, but stopped short.

"And you?" he said.

"After you. Then I'll eat."

The thick lips opened slightly. The Arab hesitated, then bit into the cake without further ado.

The meal over, the Arab looked at the schoolteacher. "Are you . . . the judge?"

"No, I'm keeping you until tomorrow."

"Why do you sit down to eat with me?"

"I'm hungry."

The Arab fell silent. Daru got up and left the room. He brought back a folding bed from the shed, set it up between the table and the stove, perpendicular to his own bed. From a large suitcase in the corner, serving as a shelf for school folders, he took two blankets and spread them on the camp bed. This done, he felt at loose ends, and sat down on his bed. There was nothing more to do or to prepare. He had to look at this man. He gazed at him, trying to imagine that face transported with rage. He was unable to. He saw only his gloomy yet shining eyes and the coarse mouth.

"Why did you kill him?" he asked in a voice whose hostile tone surprised him.

The Arab lowered his eyes.

"He ran away. I ran after him."

He looked up at Daru again and his eyes bore an expression of miserable questioning. "Now what will they do to me?"

"Are you afraid?"

The Arab stiffened, and looked away.

"Are you sorry?"

The Arab looked at him openmouthed. Obviously he did not understand. Daru was becoming irritated. At the same time he felt clumsy and ill at ease, with his big body wedged between the two beds.

"Lie down there," he said impatiently. "That's your bed."

The Arab did not move. He called out to Daru:

"Listen!"

The schoolteacher looked at him.

"Is the gendarme coming back tomorrow?"

"I don't know."

"Are you coming with us?"

"I don't know. Why?"

The prisoner got up and stretched out on top of the blankets, his feet toward the window. The light from the electric bulb shone straight into his eyes and he closed them at once.

"Why?" Daru repeated, standing beside the bed.

The Arab opened his eyes under the blinding light and looked at him, trying hard not to blink.

"Come with us," he said.

In the middle of the night Daru was still awake. He had lain down on his bed after undressing completely—he was used to sleeping naked. But now when he realized that he had no clothes on him, he was uneasy. He did not feel safe and was tempted to dress again. Then he shrugged the matter off; after all, he had been through such things before, and if attacked he could break his adversary in two. He observed the Arab from his bed, lying there on his back, still motionless, with his eyes closed against the harsh light. When Daru put out the light, the darkness seemed to thicken all at once. The night grew vivid in the window, the starless sky stirring gently. The schoolteacher could soon distinguish the stretched-out body in front of him. The Arab remained motionless, but his eyes seemed open now. A light wind prowled around the schoolhouse. It would probably chase away the clouds and the sun would return tomorrow.

The wind increased during the night. The hens fluttered a bit and then quieted down. The Arab turned over on his side with his back to Daru. Daru thought he heard him moan. He kept listening to that breathing, so close to him, and brooded, unable to fall asleep. This presence, here in the room where he had been sleeping alone for a long year, disturbed him. But it disturbed him also because it imposed on him a certain kind of brotherhood he knew well—but which he rejected in the present circumstances—the brotherhood of men sharing the same room, such as soldiers or prisoners, when they begin to feel a strange bond. Having shed their armor with their civilian clothes, they are able to gather every evening, despite their differences, in the ancient community of hope and exhaustion. But Daru shook himself; he didn't like such foolish musings, and he had to get some sleep.

Still later, however, when the Arab stirred about almost imperceptibly, the schoolteacher was still awake. When the prisoner moved a second time, he stiffened, on the alert. The Arab slowly raised himself on his arms, almost with the motion of a sleepwalker. Sitting up on his bed, he waited, motionless, without turning his head toward Daru, as if he were listening with all his attention. Daru did not move, though it had just occurred to him that the revolver was still in his desk drawer. It would be better to act right away. Yet he continued to observe the prisoner, who, with the same smooth and soundless motion lowered his feet to the floor, waited again, then began slowly to stand up. Daru was going to call out to him, when the Arab began to walk, in a natural but uncannily silent way. He went toward the back door leading into the shed. He lifted the latch with precaution and went out, pulling the door behind him, without shutting it. Daru had not stirred. "He's escaping," he merely thought. "Good riddance!" Yet he kept his ear cocked. The hens were not fluttering—he must therefore be on the plateau. A faint sound of water reached him, and he didn't understand what it was until the Arab again stood framed in the doorway, closed the door carefully, and came back to bed without a sound. Then Daru turned his back to him and fell asleep. Later, in his deep sleep, he seemed to hear stealthy steps around the schoolhouse. "I'm dreaming, I'm dreaming!" he repeated to himself. And he went on sleeping.

When he awoke, the sky was clear; the loosely fitting window let in a stream of cold and pure air. The Arab was asleep, curled up under the blankets now, his mouth open, completely relaxed. But when Daru shook him, he jumped with terror, staring wildly at Daru without recognizing him and with such an expression of panic that the schoolteacher drew back. "Don't be afraid. It's me. You must get up and have something to eat." The Arab nodded his head and said yes. He was calm again but his expression was vacant and listless.

The coffee was ready. They drank it, both seated on the folding bed and munching their pieces of flat cake. Then Daru led the Arab to the shed and showed him the faucet where he washed. He went back into the room, folded up the blankets and the bed, made his own bed, and put the room in order. Then he went out onto the terrace through the classroom. The sun was already rising in the blue sky; a soft and radiant light was bathing the barren plateau. On the slope the snow was melting here and there. The stones were about to reappear. Crouched on the edge of the plateau, the schoolteacher contemplated the arid expanse. He thought of Balducci. He had hurt the man's feelings, he had sent him off brusquely, seeming indifferent to his predicament. He could still hear the tone of the gendarme's good-by, and, without knowing the reason for it, he felt strangely hollow and vulnerable. At that moment, from the other side of the schoolhouse, he heard the prisoner cough. Daru listened to him almost despite himself, and then, furious, he flung a pebble, sending it whistling through the air before it sank into the snow. The stupid crime the man had committed revolted him, but to hand him over was dishonorable—the mere thought of it made him fume with indignation. And he cursed both his own people who had sent him this Arab and the Arab himself who had had the nerve to kill but had not known how to escape. Daru got up, walked in a circle over the terrace, stood stock-still for a moment, then went back to the schoolhouse.

The Arab, bending over the cement floor of the shed, was washing his teeth with two fingers. Daru looked at him, then said, "Come." He returned to his room, walking ahead of the prisoner. He put on a hunting jacket over his sweater and pulled on his walking shoes. He stood up and waited for the Arab to get into his *chèche* and sandals. They walked into the classroom and the schoolteacher pointed to the exit. "Go," he said. The other didn't move. "I'm coming with you," said Daru. The Arab went out. Daru returned to his room, where he made a package of pieces of rusk, some dates, and sugar. Back in the classroom, before leaving, he hesitated a second in front of his desk, then crossed the school threshold and locked the door.

"We go this way," he said, and started out eastward, followed by the prisoner. When they were but a short distance from the schoolhouse, he thought he heard a slight sound behind him. He retraced his steps and inspected the grounds around the building; there was no one there. The Arab watched him without seeming to understand. "Let's go," Daru said.

They walked for an hour then rested beside a jagged limestone. The snow was melting ever faster, with the sun sucking up the puddles at once and rapidly clearing the plateau, which gradually dried and vibrated like the air itself. When they resumed walking, the newly bared ground rang under their feet. Now and then a bird rent the air in front of them with a joyful cry. Daru drank in the fresh morning radiance with deep breaths. A kind of exaltation rose in him before the familiar vast expanse, almost all of it yellow now under the vault of blue sky. They walked another hour, descending toward the south. They reached a sort of flat-topped elevation covered with crumbling rock. From there the plateau sloped eastward, toward a low plain with a few sparse trees. To the south it sloped toward masses of rock, which gave the landscape a chaotic look.

Daru scanned both directions. There was nothing but the sky on the horizon—there was no sign of man. He turned to the Arab, who was staring at him blankly. Daru held out the parcel to him. "Take it," he said, "they're dates, bread, and sugar—they'll last you for two days. Here are a thousand francs too." The Arab took the parcel and the money; he held them at chest level, as if he didn't know what to do with what had just been given him. "Now look," the schoolteacher said, pointing east, "that's the way to Tinguit. It's a two hours' walk. The administration and the police are at Tinguit—they're expecting you." The Arab looked in the direction in which Daru was pointing, still holding the parcel and the money against his chest. Daru took him by the arm and turned him, not gently, toward the south. At the foot of the elevation on which they were standing, the faint markings of a path could be discerned. "That's the trail across the plateau. In a day's distance from here you'll find pasturelands and the first nomads. They'll welcome you and give you shelter, as is their custom."

The Arab had now turned toward Daru, his face expressing a sort of panic. "Listen," he said.

Daru shook his head, "No, don't speak. I'm going to leave you now." He turned away, took two long strides in the direction of the school, looked around hesitantly at the motionless Arab, and started off again. For a few minutes he heard nothing but his own footsteps against the cold earth, and he did not turn his head. A moment later, however, he turned around. The Arab was still standing there, on the crest of the hill, his arms hanging at his sides now, and he was looking at the schoolteacher. Daru felt a lump in his throat. But he swore, waved his arm with impatience, and started off again. After walking some distance, he again stopped and looked. There was no one on the hill now.

Daru hesitated. The sun was quite high in the sky and was beginning to beat down on his head. He retraced his steps, at first somewhat uncertainly, then with determination. By the time he reached the little hill his body was streaming with sweat. He climbed it as fast as he could and stopped, out of breath, at the top. The fields of rock to the south were clearly outlined against the blue sky, but on the plain to the east a heat-haze was already rising. And in that light haze, Daru, with heavy heart, made out the Arab walking slowly along the road to prison.

A little later, standing in front of the classroom window, the schoolteacher was watching the clear light rise over the whole plateau, but he hardly saw it. Behind him on the blackboard, across the winding French rivers, stretched the words clumsily written with chalk, which he had just read: "You handed over our brother. You will pay for this." Daru looked at the sky, the plateau, and beyond, at the invisible regions stretching all the way to the sea. In this vast land he had so loved, he was alone.

1513010

CRAINQUEBILLE

Anatole France

ANATOLE FRANCE, who made his world reputation in the early part of this century, received the Nobel award in 1921. He continues to be regarded as a brilliant artist in the French language. In the words of one critic, "His style, pure as spring water, is flavored with delicate irony." Born in 1844, Anatole France produced in his long life (he died in 1924), a vast number of works as novelist, historian, biographer, poet, and short-story writer. He attained his first success with the novel, *The Crime of Sylvester Bonnard,* and continued to delight his readers with his sophistication, wide erudition, sensitivity to beauty, and exquisite humor and irony.

Then came the upheaval of the Dreyfus case and the storm of protest in France and in all other civilized countries against its anti-Semitism. Alfred Dreyfus (1859–1935), a French artillery officer of Jewish lineage, was charged, in 1894, with selling military secrets to Germany. He was sentenced to the notorious Devil's Island for life. It was soon proved that some of the "evidence" used against him had been forged. The retrial was a mockery, and he was found guilty a second time. Under the leadership of Émile Zola, a number of other prominent French authors, Anatole France among them, threw themselves into the drawn-out crusade to gain Dreyfus' exoneration and freedom.

Anatole France abandoned his former preference for serene and refined wit and began to produce fiction and fantasy with satirical bite against intolerance, judicial dishonesty, and superstition. Consequently, it was in this period that he wrote the satirical novels *Penguin Island* and *The Revolt of the Angels,* as well as his famous story, "Crainquebille," in which he satirizes the cumbersome and callous French courts and what happens to a poor pushcart peddler who falls into the clutches of "the majesty of justice."

CRAINQUEBILLE

The entire majesty of justice dwells in every sentence meted out by a judge in the name of the sovereign people. Jérôme Crainquebille, pushcart peddler of vegetables, experienced the awesome character of that justice when, charged with having insulted an officer of public safety, he appeared in court. Seated in the offender's chair, in the magnificent and somber chamber, he looked at the magistrates, the clerks, the lawyers in their robes, the usher wearing his chain, the guards, and, on the other side of a railing, the bared heads of the silent spectators.

So conspicuous on his raised seat in the dock, facing the magistrates, the accused saw himself as singled out for a grim honor. Presiding Judge Bourriche sat at the end of the chamber, between two assessors. The palm leaves of an officer of the Academy were pinned to his chest. Above the judge's tribunal were a bust of Marianne, representing the republic, and a Crucifix, so that all laws, divine and human, seemed to threaten Crainquebille's fate. He was terrified by these symbols. And not having a philosophical turn of mind, he did not wonder about the meaning of the bust and the Crucifix, nor did he seek to discover whether Jesus and Marianne were in accord about what went on in law courts. Yet these were matters for reflection. For, after all, pontifical doctrine and canon law are on many points in disagreement with the constitution of the republic and with the Civil Code. The Church of Christ teaches today, as formerly, that only those powers are lawful to which it has given its sanction. The French Republic claims to be free from pontifical power, however. Crainquebille might therefore have said, with some reason:

"Gentlemen magistrates, inasmuch as President Loubet of our republic has not been anointed, the Christ who is suspended over our heads repudiates you through his spokesmen of councils and of popes. Either He is here to remind you of the prerogatives of the Church, which annul yours, or His presence here has no rational significance."

To which Presiding Judge Bourriche might have replied:

"Prisoner Crainquebille, the kings of France have always been on bad terms with the pope. Guillaume de Nogaret was excommunicated, but resign his office he did not, for so petty a reason. No, the Christ over this tribune is not the Christ of Gregory VII or of Boniface VIII.* He is, if you please, the Christ of the Gospels, who knew not one word of canon law."

Then Crainquebille might justifiably have answered:

"The Christ of the Gospels was a rebel. Besides, He was the victim of a sentence which for nineteen hundred years all Christian peoples have considered as a grave judicial error. I defy Your Honor to condemn me in His name even to as much as only forty-eight hours of imprisonment.

* Gregory VII (Pope from 1073 to 1085) and Boniface VIII (Pope from 1294 to 1303) had insisted on papal supremacy in secular affairs. They were successfully defied by kings Henry IV of England and Philip of France, respectively.

But Crainquebille did not indulge in any historical, political, or social considerations. He sat there stupified with amazement. On the contrary, the ritual with which he was surrounded gave him a very lofty idea of justice. Overcome with awe, sunk in terror, he was ready to defer to his judges in the matter of his guilt. In his own conscience he did not believe that he was a criminal; but he knew how trivial is the conscience of a vegetable vendor in the face of the considerations of the law and the ministers of public prosecution. Already his lawyer had half-persuaded him that he was not innocent.

A brief and hurried summation had established the charges that now bore down upon him.

CRAINQUEBILLE'S STORY

Jérôme Crainquebille, vegetable hawker, pushed his cart up and down the streets of the city, crying, *Cabbages! Turnips! Carrots!* And when he had leeks he cried, *Bunches of Asparagus*—for leeks are the asparagus of the poor. Now it happened that on the twentieth day of October, at the noon hour, as he was going down the Rue Montmartre, the shoemaker's wife, Madame Bayard, came out of her shop and approached Crainquebille's vegetable cart. Disdainfully picking up a bunch of leeks, she said:

"They are not too good, your leeks. How much a bunch?"

"Fifteen sous, ma'am, and there are none better."

"Fifteen sous for three miserable leeks?" And she threw the leeks back with a gesture of disgust.

It was at that moment that Policeman ✗64 came up and said to Crainquebille:

"Move along."

As for moving along, that was what Crainquebille had been doing from morning till dark for fifty years now. Such an order, therefore, seemed proper to him and in accordance with the nature of things. So, fully prepared to obey, he urged the woman to hurry and take what was to her liking.

"Give me a chance to choose what I want," the shoemaker's wife retorted sourly.

And she fingered every bunch of leeks all over again, finally selected the one she thought the best, and held it clasped to her bosom, as saints in church paintings hold the holy palm.

"I'll give you fourteen sous. That's plenty. But I'll have to get it from the shop, for I don't have any money on me."

Still hugging the leeks, she returned to the shoemaker's shop, into which a customer carrying a child had preceded her.

Right at this moment Policeman ⚹64 said to Crainquebille for the second time:

"Move along."

"I'm waiting for my money," replied Crainquebille.

"I'm not telling you to wait for your money; I'm telling you to move along," said the policeman sternly.

Meanwhile, the shoemaker's wife was fitting blue slippers on an eighteen-month child; its mother was in a hurry. And the green heads of the leeks were resting on the counter.

For the half century that he had been pushing his cart through the streets, Crainquebille had learned to obey the representatives of authority. But this time he found himself in a peculiar position—between that which was his duty and what was his right. His was not a judical mind. He did not understand that the exercise of an individual's right did not free him from the obligation to comply with social duty. He gave too great a consideration to his right to receive the fourteen sous and too little to his duty to push his cart and move along, always move along. He opted to stay where he was.

For the third time Policeman ⚹64, quietly and without rancor, ordered him to leave. Unlike police sergeant Montauciel, who had a way of constantly threatening but never preferring charges, Policeman ※64 was slow to threaten and quick to act. Such was his nature. Though somewhat devious, he was an excellent public servant and a loyal soldier. He had the courage of a lion and the gentleness of a child. He considered nothing but his official duty.

"Don't you understand?—I told you to move along."

Crainquebille had too good a reason for not budging, and he considered this reason quite sufficient. He stated it simply and artlessly:

"Good Lord! Didn't I tell you that I'm waiting for my money?"

Policeman ※64 merely replied: "Do you want me to take you in? If you do, just say so."

At these words Crainquebille slowly shrugged his shoulders, stared sadly at the policeman, and raised his eyes to heaven as if to say:

"May God be my witness! Do I scorn the law? Do I laugh at all the bylaws and ordinances which regulate my ambulatory trade? At five o'clock this morning I was already at the Halles market square. Since seven, pushing my cart and working my hands to the bone, I've been crying: *Cabbages! Turnips! Carrots!* I am sixty. I am worn out. And you ask me whether I am raising the black flag of revolt! You are laughing at me, and cruel is your mockery."

Either because he did not notice the expression on Crainquebille's face, or because he thought it no excuse for disobedience, the policeman asked curtly and harshly whether he had been understood.

It so happened that the traffic in the Rue Montmartre was at its worst at that hour. Cabs, drays, carts, omnibuses, trucks were jammed one against the other, seeming indissolubly joined together. And over their restless immobility rose many oaths and shouts. Cabmen and butcher's boys swapped eloquent insults from a distance, and the omnibus drivers, perceiving Crainquebille as the cause of the impasse, called him a "dirty leek."

Meanwhile a crowd of the curious had gathered on the sidewalk to listen to the dispute. Finding himself the center of attention, the policeman had no other thought than to display his authority.

"Very well, you asked for it," he said, taking a greasy notepad and a stubby pencil from his pocket.

Crainquebille stuck to his guns, obedient to an inner voice. Besides, it was now impossible for him to move on or to move back. Unfortunately, the wheel of his pushchart was caught in the wheel of the milkman's vehicle.

Lifting his cap, he tore his hair, and cried: "But haven't I been telling you that I'm waiting for my money? Don't you see the fix I'm in?"

These words, which Crainquebille employed to express despair rather than insurrection, Policeman ⚹64 considered insulting. And, since to his mind all insults to members of his calling must necessarily be couched in the traditional, consecrated, ritual, and, thus, liturgical form of *"Mort aux vaches!"* (Down with stool pigeons!) it was thus that he heard and understood the offender's words.

"Ah! you said 'Mort aux vaches!' Very well. Come along."

Crainquebille, shocked and distressed by the turn of events, fixed his large feverish eyes on Policeman ⚹64. In a broken voice emerging now from the top of his head, now from under his heels, and with his arms folded over his blue smock, he screamed:

"I said 'Mort aux vaches?' Me? Oh! . . ."

The arrest was hailed with laughter by the clerks and the errand boys. It satisfied in them the taste that all crowds have for mean and violent scenes. But one person pushed his way through the mob—a sad-looking gentleman dressed in black and wearing a top hat. He went up to the policeman and said to him mildly but firmly:

"You are mistaken. This man did not insult you."

"Mind your own business," the policeman retorted, but since the man was well dressed, he didn't threaten him.

The old gentleman persisted calmly but tenaciously. The policeman ordered him to make his statement to the commissioner.

Meanwhile Crainquebille was exclaiming:

"So, you're still saying that I said 'Mort aux vaches!' Oh! . . ."

He was shouting these words of consternation when Madame Bayard, the shoemaker's wife, came over to the cart with the fourteen sous in her hand. But Policeman ⚡64 already had Crainquebille by the collar, and Madame Bayard, convinced that one owed nothing to a man who was being taken to the police station, put the fourteen sous into her apron pocket.

And, realizing suddenly that his pushcart had been confiscated, that he had lost his freedom, that an abyss of misfortune was opening up before him, and that his sun was setting, Crainquebille murmured resignedly:

"*Tout de même!* . . . Well, that's how it goes! . . ."

The old gentleman later declared before the commissioner that having been hindered on his way by the traffic jam, he had witnessed the incident and could affirm that the policeman had not been insulted, that he was totally mistaken. He gave his name and profession: David Matthieu, chief physician at the Ambroise-Paré Hospital, officer of the Legion of Honor. At any other time, such evidence would have convinced the commissioner. But men of science were currently suspect in France.

Crainquebille remained under arrest, spent the night in a police-station cell, and in the morning was transferred to prison in a paddy wagon.

Prison did not seem to him sad or humiliating. It seemed

to him inevitable. What struck him as he entered was the cleanliness of the walls and of the brick floor.

"It sure is a clean place," he remarked to himself. "Couldn't be cleaner. You could eat off the floor."

When he was left alone, he wanted to pull out his stool; but he noticed that it was fastened to the wall. He expressed his surprise aloud:

"What a funny idea! Now there's something I'd never have thought of."

He sat down, twiddled his thumbs, and remained lost in amazement. The silence and the solitude overwhelmed him. But he soon felt bored and began to think about his push-cart, which had been confiscated with its load of cabbages, carrots, celery, lamb's lettuce, and dandelions. He wondered with alarm, "Where have they done away with my cart?"

On the third day his lawyer called on him—Mr. Lemerle, one of the youngest members of the Paris Bar, president of one of the branches of the League for the French Father-land.

Crainquebille endeavored to tell him his story, which was not easy to do. He was not used to talking. For all that, with a little help he might perhaps have succeeded. But his lawyer shook his head doubtfully at everything he said, and, leafing through his papers, he muttered:

"Hmm, hmm . . . I don't see anything about all this in my brief." Finally, in a bored tone he said, twirling his blond mustache:

"It would probably be preferable, in your own interest, for you to confess. In my opinion your obstinacy in insisting on absolute denial is downright stupid."

And from that point on, Crainquebille would have made a confession if he had only known what he was supposed to confess.

CRAINQUEBILLE BEFORE THE TRIBUNAL OF JUSTICE

Presiding Judge Bourriche gave six full minutes to the examination of Crainquebille. This examination would have been more illuminating if the accused had replied to the questions posed to him. But he was not experienced in argument, and in the presence of such personages, reverence and fear sealed his lips. The accused maintained silence, and the presiding judge answered his own questions. And his replies to them were overwhelming. He said in conclusion: "At last, you do admit having said 'Mort aux vaches!'"

"I said 'Mort aux vaches' because the policeman had said 'Mort aux vaches,' so then I said 'Mort aux vaches.'"

What the accused meant to say was that, being astounded by this most unexpected of accusations, he had, in his stupefaction, merely repeated the words so falsely attributed to him—words that he had most definitely not uttered. He had said "Mort aux vaches" as if to say, "Me, utter such words! How could you think such a thing?"

Presiding Judge Bourriche did not see the matter in the same light.

"Do you mean to say," he asked, "that it was the policeman who first uttered the insult?"

Crainquebille gave up trying to explain himself. It was too difficult for him.

"I see you do not insist on your contention. You are right not to do so," opined the presiding judge.

And he had the witnesses called.

Policeman ✕64, Bastien Matra by name, swore to tell the truth and nothing but the truth. Then he testified as follows:

"I was on duty on October 20, at noon, when I noticed in the Rue Montmartre a person who appeared to be a street vendor unlawfully standing with his pushcart opposite number 328, this causing a traffic obstruction. Three times I gave him the order to move along, but he refused to obey. And when I warned him that I was about to charge him, he responded by crying, 'Mort aux vaches!' which sounded to me like an insult."

This evidence, presented in a firm and moderate tone, was heard with obvious approbation by the tribunal. The witnesses for the defense were Madame Bayard, the shoemaker's wife, and Dr. David Matthieu, chief phyiscian of the Ambroise-Paré Hospital, officer of the Legion of Honor. Madame Bayard had seen and heard nothing. Dr. Matthieu had been in the crowd which had gathered around the policeman ordering the peddler to move on. His evidence led to a new development in the trial.

"I witnessed the incident," he said. "I observed that the policeman had made a mistake—he had not been insulted. I went over to him and said so. However, the policeman continued to hold the peddler under arrest, suggesting that I follow him to the commissioner, which I did. I repeated my declaration before the commissioner."

"You may sit down," said the presiding judge. "Usher, recall witness Matra."

"Matra, when you proceeded to arrest the accused, did not Dr. Matthieu point out to you that you were mistaken?"

"The fact is, your honor, he, too, insulted me."

"What did he say?"

"He said 'Mort aux vaches!' "

A murmur and laughter rose in the courtroom. "That will do," said the presiding judge, hastily dismissing the witness.

And he warned the public that if such unseemly demonstrations occurred again, he would clear the court. Meanwhile, the counsel for the defense was triumphantly fluttering the sleeves of his gown, and it seemed for the moment that Crainquebille would be acquitted.

Order having been restored, Defense Attorney Lemerle rose. He opened his plea with a eulogy of policemen: ". . . those self-effacing servants of society who, in return for an insignificant salary, suffer fatigue and face constant perils with daily heroism. They were once soldiers, and soldiers they remain. 'Soldiers!'—that word expresses everything . . ."

And from this observation, Lemerle went on to hold forth with ease and eloquence on the virtues of the military. He was one of those, he said, who would not allow a finger to be laid on the army, on that national army of which he was proud to be a part.

The presiding judge bowed. Lemerle was, in fact a lieutenant in the reserves. He was also a nationalist candidate for the Les Vieilles Haudriettes subdistrict. Pursuing the subject, he went on:

"No, I most assuredly do not fail to recognize the invaluable and self-effacing services daily rendered the valiant people of Paris by the guardians of the peace. And I should not have consented to defend Crainquebille before you, gentlemen, had I beheld in him a man who had insulted a former soldier. My client is accused of having said 'Mort aux vaches!' The meaning of this expression is not ambiguous. If you leaf through *Le Dictionnaire de la Langue Verte* (the dictionary of slang), you will find: '*Vachard*,' a sluggard, an idler, one who lounges lazily like a cow instead of working. '*Vache*,' one who sells himself to the police—a police spy. Obviously, 'Mort aux vaches' is an expression used by a certain type of worthless person. But the whole matter resolves itself here into this: how did Crainquebille say it? And, further, did he say it at all? Permit me, gentlemen, to doubt it.

"I do not suspect Policeman Matra of any malicious intent. But, as we have said, he performs difficult tasks. He is there-

fore sometimes fatigued, harassed, overtaxed. In such a state
he could have been the victim of a sort of hallucination of the
ear. But, when he appears before you, gentleman, and tells
you that the good doctor David Matthieu, officer of the Legion
of Honor, chief physician at the Ambroise-Paré Hospital a
prince of science and a man of the world, said to him 'Mort
aux vaches!'——then we are inevitably forced to conclude that
Matra is a prey to obsession, and if the term is not too
strong, to delusions of persecution.

"And even if Crainquebille had cried 'Mort aux vaches!'
it would remain to be ascertained whether this expression,
coming from his lips, would constitute an offense. Crainquebille happens to be the natural child of a woman vegetable
hawker; he has been ruined by years of depravity and drunkenness; indeed, he was born an alcoholic. You behold him
brutalized by sixty years of destitution. Gentlemen, you will
perceive that he is irresponsible."

Attorney Lemerle sat down. Then Presiding Judge Bourriche muttered a sentence, condemning Jérôme Crainquebille
to a fortnight in prison and a fine of fifty francs. The tribunal
based the conviction on the evidence given by Policeman
Matra.

As he was being led down the long somber corridor of
the Palace of Justice, Crainquebille felt a keen need for human sympathy. He turned to the Municipal Guard of Paris
who was escorting him and called out to him three times:

"Oh, 'Cipal! . . . 'Cipal! . . . 'Cipal!" he sighed. "If anyone had said to me only a fortnight ago that this was going to
happen to Crainquebille! . . ."

Then he made the observation, "They speak too fast, those
gentlemen. They speak well, but too fast. And you can't
make them understand you . . . 'Cipal, don't you agree that
they speak too fast?"

But the soldier walked straight ahead without replying or
even turning his head.

Crainquebille asked him:

"Why don't you answer me?"

The soldier kept silent. And Crainquebille said to him bitterly:

"People speak even to a dog. Why not speak to me? Don't you ever open your mouth? Is it because your breath stinks?"

CRAINQUEBILLE SUBMITS
TO THE LAWS OF THE REPUBLIC

Having been brought back to the prison cell, Crainquebille sat down on his chained stool, to think. He was filled with astonishment and admiration. He had no inkling that the judges had made a mistake. The tribunal had concealed its essential weaknesses behind the majesty of its procedures. Nor could he conceive that he might be right as against the magistrates. Although he failed to understand their reason for sentencing him, it was impossible for him to believe that anything could go wrong in so handsome a ceremony. For, never having attended Mass or visited the Élysée, Crainquebille had never before in his life witnessed anything so splendid as a police-court trial.

He knew very well that he had not cried "Mort aux vaches!" And, that he had been condemned to fifteen days in prison for having cried these words, seemed to him an awesome mystery, one of those articles of faith to which believers adhere without understanding them, as something unfathomable, striking, delightful, and awe inspiring.

The poor old man believed himself guilty of having mystically offended Policeman ⚹64, just as the little boy who learns his catechism believes himself guilty of Eve's sin. His arrest signified that he had cried "Mort aux vaches!" He must therefore have indeed cried "Mort aux vaches!" in some occult way obscure to himself. And, by virtue of this, he felt himself transported to a supernatural world. His trial was his apocalypse.

Crainquebille had only a vague idea of his offense, but his idea of the penalty was no clearer. His sentence seemed to him a solemn and high ritual, dazzling and beyond comprehension, something not to be questioned, and for which he could neither be proud nor complain. Indeed, if at that moment he saw Judge Bourriche with a halo around his head and white wings on his back descend through an opening in the ceiling, he would not have been surprised at such additional manifestation of judicial glory. He would have told himself, "This is my trial continuing."

On the next day his lawyer came to see him:

"Well, my good fellow, things didn't turn out too badly for you after all, did they? Don't you be discouraged! Two weeks pass quickly. No, we haven't much to complain about."

"As for that, I can say that the gentlemen were quite pleasant to me, quite polite; not a single rude word. I wouldn't have believed it. And the 'Cipal wore white gloves for the occasion. Did you notice?"

"Everything considered, we did well to confess."

"Perhaps."

"Crainquebille, I have some good news to report to you. A charitable person whom I had interested in your plight gave me the sum of fifty francs for you which will go toward your fine."

"When will you give me the fifty?"

"It will be paid to the clerk. Don't you worry about it."

"I suppose that's just as good. All the same, I thank this person." And Crainquebille murmured pensively, "It's not an ordinary thing, what's happening to me!"

"Don't exaggerate, Crainquebille. Your case is by no means rare, far from it."

"Could you perhaps tell me where they've hid my push-cart?"

CRAINQUEBILLE EXPOSED TO PUBLIC OPINION

After leaving prison, Crainquebille resumed pushing his cart along the Rue Montmartre, crying, *Cabbages! Turnips! Carrots!* He was neither proud nor ashamed of his adventure. The memory of it was not painful. He stored it in his mind with impressions of the theater, of travel, and of dreams. But, above all, he was glad to be walking in the mud, along the paved streets, and again to see, overhead, the sky, wet and dirty as the guttered streams—the good sky of his city. He would stop at every corner to buy himself a drink; then, feeling free and gay, he would spit in his hands in order to moisten his calloused palms, grasp the shafts and push his cart. A flight of sparrows, early risers also and as poor as he— seeking their livelihood in the gutter—flew off at the sound of his familiar cry, *Cabbages! Turnips! Carrots!* An old house-wife came over and said to him, as she felt his celery:

"What's happened to you, Crainquebille? You haven't been around for three weeks. Have you been sick? You look a little pale."

"To tell you the truth, Madame Mailloche, I've been living the life of a landowner . . ."

Nothing changed for him, except that he went more often to the wineshops, because he felt in a holiday mood since his release from prison. In this mood he also had the idea that he was getting to know lots of kindly folk there. He would return to his garret in a rather gay state. He would stretch out on his mattress, cover himself with the sacks lent to him by the corner chestnut vendor—they served him as a blanket —and lie there musing, "Prison isn't so bad. You have everything you need there. But just the same it is better to be in your own home."

His contentment was not of long duration, however. He soon noticed that his customers were shunning him.

"I've got some fine celery, Madame Cointreau!"

"I don't need anything."

"What do you mean you don't need anything? Do you live on air these days?"

And Madame Cointreau, without replying, returned haughtily to the large bakery, of which she was the owner. The shopkeepers and the concièrges, who not long ago constantly came around to his pushcart, all green and blooming, now turned away from him. Having reached the shoemaker's at the sign of the Guardian Angel, the spot where his judicial misadventures had begun, he called out:

"Madame Bayard, Madame Bayard, you owe me fifteen sous from last time."

But Madame Bayard, who was sitting at her counter, did not deign to turn her head.

The whole of Rue Montmartre knew that old man Crainquebille had been in jail, and the whole of Rue Montmartre no longer wanted to know him. Rumors of his imprisonment spread to the end of the Montmartre neighborhood and the tumultuous corner of the Rue Richer. There, one day, at about noon, he noticed Madame Laure, a good and faithful customer, leaning over the cart of another vegetable peddler, young Martin. She was feeling a large cabbage. Her hair glistened in the sun like skeins of loosely wound golden thread. And young Martin, a nobody, a dirty bum, was swearing with his hand on his heart that there were no finer vegetables than his. At this sight, Crainquebille's heart was about to break. He pushed his cart alongside Martin's and said to Madame Laure in a plaintive, quavering voice:

"It's not nice of you to be unfaithful to me."

Madame Laure, as she herself admitted, was no duchess. It was not in high society that she had obtained her knowledge of the paddy wagon and police cell. But one can insist on being proper no matter what one's station in life—isn't that true? Everyone has his self-respect; and who likes to have dealings with a man who has just come out of prison? She responded to Crainquebille's words with a look of revulsion. And the old pushcart peddler, resenting the affront, blurted out:

"You dirty wench, get out of my sight!"

Madame Laure dropped her green cabbage and cried:

"You get away from here, you old jailbird! That thing comes out of jail and has the nerve to start insulting people!"

Had Crainquebille possessed greater composure, he would never have reproached Madame Laure with her calling. He knew only too well that one could not always do what he preferred in life, one could not always choose his occupation, and that there were good people to be found everywhere. In the past he had been careful, and wisely ignored his customers' private business; and he had looked down on no one. But at the moment he was beside himself. He proceeded to insult Madame Laure in three separate ways, by calling her a filthy wench, a carrion, a harridan. The curious gathered around Madame Laure and Crainquebille and listened to them exchange a few additional insults, as solemn as the first. And the two would soon have used up their entire stock of epithets had not a policeman suddenly appeared. With his silent immobility he rendered them as silent and as motionless as himself. The two separated. But this scene resulted in lowering Crainquebille still further in the eyes of the inhabitants of the Montmartre neighborhood and the Rue Richer.

THE CONSEQUENCES

The old man walked away mumbling:

"She's nothing but a hussy. And there's no worse hussy than that woman!"

But deep in his heart that was not what he reproached her for. He did not condemn her for being what she was. He

even esteemed her, knowing that she was frugal and stable.
In the past they had liked to chat. She used to tell him about
her parents who lived in the country. And they had each
planned to cultivate a small garden and raise poultry. She had
been a good customer. And to see her now buying cabbages
from that young Martin, that filthy specimen of a good-for-
nothing, made Crainquebille sick to his stomach. Worse, she
put on airs and treated him with contempt—that was too
much, and, well . . .

Alas, she was not the only one who treated him like a
mangy dog! No one wanted to have anything to do with
him. Just like Madame Laure, Madame Cointreau the baker,
Madame Bayard of the Guardian Angel, scorned and
avoided him. In fact, the whole community shunned him.

So! Because he had been locked up for a fortnight was he
no longer good enough even to sell leeks? Was that just? Did
it make any sense to cause a decent man to die of hunger
because he had gotten into trouble with a cop? If he could no
longer sell vegetables, he might as well be dead.

Like a badly aged wine he turned sour. After having had
"words" with Madame Laure, he began to have them with
everyone. At the least provocation he would tell his customers
the truth about themselves—and, you can well believe it,
he did not handle them with silk gloves. If they happened to
feel his wares a little too long, he would call them to their
faces fumblers and softheads. And at the bistros he would
abuse his companions. His friend the chestnut vendor would
no longer have anything to do with him, declaring that Crainquebille had turned into a damned old porcupine. There was
no denying it—he had indeed become a coarse, disagreeable,
evil-mouthed person, and a gabbler to boot. The truth of
the matter was that, having discovered the imperfections of
society, he lacked the poise of a professor of moral and political science in expressing his views on the vices of the system

and the needed reforms; his thoughts did not emerge in words of order and moderation.

Misfortune was rendering him unfair. He was taking his revenge on those who did not wish him ill, and sometimes on those who were weaker than he. One day he slapped Alphonse, the wineseller's small son, because he had asked him whether jail was a pleasant place. Crainquebille struck him, saying:

"Filthy brat! It's your father who ought to be locked up and not be free to enrich himself by selling poison."

An action and a speech which did him no honor. For, as the chestnut vendor justly pointed out, one must not strike a child, nor reproach him with a father whom he has not chosen.

Crainquebille began to drink. The less money he earned, the more brandy he drank. Up to now frugal and sober, he was astounded at the change in him.

"I never used to be a reveler," he told himself. "I guess you become less sensible as you grow older."

Sometimes he blamed himself severely for his misconduct and his laziness: "Crainquebille, old man, you're good for nothing but bending the elbow."

Sometimes he fooled himself, pretending that he drank out of desperation. "I must have a glass from time to time— I must drink to give me a little strength and to revive my spirits. Something burns inside me, and there's nothing like drink to quench it."

It often happened now that he missed the early-morning auction at the market and had to buy damaged produce, which they let him have on credit. One day, feeling weary and down-hearted, he left his pushcart in its shed and spent the whole blessed day hanging around the stall of Madame Rose, the tripe vendor, and going in and out of the neighborhood bistros near the Halles market. In the evening, seated on a basket, he meditated and realized how low he had sunk. He recalled his

youthful strength and labors, and his good earnings. He remembered those days without number, all alike and busy.
He thought back to how he used to pace at dawn, waiting
for the early-market auction; the vegetables carried by the
armful and tastefully arranged in the cart; Mama Théodore's
black coffee which he swallowed piping hot and in one gulp;
the shafts of his cart grasped firmly, and then his vigorous cry,
as loud as a cock's crow, piercing the morning air as he passed
through the crowded streets. That simple and rough life of
the human workhorse rose before him. Yes, for half a century, on his rolling stall, he had brought to people, worn
with searing labors and care, the fresh harvest of kitchen
gardens. Shaking his head he sighed:

"No! Gone is the old zest. I'm finished. The pitcher goes
so often to the well that at last it returns home broken. Come
to think of it, I've never been the same since my affair with
the court. In fact, I'm no longer the man I was."

In other words, Crainquebille was demoralized. And a
man in such a state is like one who has fallen to the ground
and is unable to rise. The passers-by step all over him.

THE ULTIMATE CONSEQUENCES

Poverty came, black poverty. The old pushcart peddler who
used to return home from Montmartre after a day's hawk-
ing with a bagful of one hundred sou pieces, now possessed
not a single coin. It was wintertime. Thrown out of his garret, he slept in a shed under the carts. The rains had been
pouring down for many days; the gutters were overflowing,
and the shed was flooded.

Crouching in his pushcart to avoid the contaminated waters, and in the company of spiders, rats, and famished cats,
he meditated in the gloom. He had eaten nothing all day,
and he no longer had the chestnut vendor's sacks to keep
him warm. Recalling the two weeks when the government

had provided him with food and warmth, he envied the lot
of prisoners, who suffer neither from cold nor hunger, and
an idea occurred to him:

"Since I know the trick, why not make good use of it?" he
told himself.

He got up and went out into the street. It was a little
after eleven. The night was bitter cold and black. A drizzling
mist was falling, colder and more penetrating than rain. The
few passers-by crept along close to the houses.

Crainquebille walked past the Church of Saint Eustache
and turned into Rue Montmartre. The street was deserted.
A guardian of the peace was standing motionless on the sidewalk near the apse of the church, under the gaslight. A fine
rain was coming down now, looking reddish around the flame.
It was falling on the policeman's cowl. The man looked
numb with the cold. But because he was tired of walking, he
remained standing near the lamp post—or, perhaps, the light
seemed a companion, a friend. The flickering flame was his
only distraction in the loneliness of the night. His immobility
made him seem not quite human; the reflections of his boots
on the wet pavement, which looked like a lake, created the
illusion of his height stretching downward, giving him from a
distance the aspect of some amphibious monster halfway out of
water. At closer range, cowled and armed, he looked both
monkish and military. The heavy features of his face, rendered even heavier under the shadow of his hood, were placid
and sad. He wore a heavy mustache, short and gray. He was
an old flatfoot, a man in his late forties. Crainquebille went
up to him warily and said in a hesitating voice:

"Mort aux vaches!"

Then he waited for the result of those hallowed words.
But nothing happened. The policeman remained motionless
and silent, his arms folded under his short cape. His wide-
open eyes glistened in the darkness and regarded Crainquebille with sadness, caution, and scorn.

Crainquebille, astonished but still determined, stammered: "I said to you 'Mort aux vaches!' "

There was a long silence in the falling of the fine red rain and in the frigid night. At last the old policeman spoke:

"One must not say such things. For certain such things are not to be said. At your age you ought to know better. Be on your way."

"Why don't you arrest me?" asked Crainquebille.

The policeman shook his head under his wet cowl:

"If we were to arrest all the drunks who say what they shouldn't, we'd never get through! And what purpose would it serve?"

Staggered by such generous disdain, Crainquebille remained standing there in the gutter, dumfounded and silent. Before going he attempted to explain:

"I didn't mean to say it to you—'Mort aux vaches!'—it was no more meant for you than for the other one. It was only for a certain reason . . ."

The policeman replied sternly, but with kindness:

"Whether it was for a reason or anything else, it shouldn't be said, because when a man does his job and endures many hardships, he ought not to be insulted with idle words. I tell you again to be on your way."

Crainquebille, head bent and arms hanging limp at his sides, plunged into the rain and the night's gloom.

PUTOIS

Anatole France

ANATOLE FRANCE's earlier style and literary preoccupations are evident in "Putois." Here he relishes leisurely digressions to characters and situations in remote works of literature, in mythology, and he even calls up the ghosts of hobgoblins. Monsieur Bergeret, a learned and witty gentleman whom the author uses as his spokesman in "Putois" (and in a number of other narratives), tells this as a story of his childhood. But beneath the playful irony and gentle mockery of the provincial mentality, the author exposes the ignorance, meanness, and superstition which cause only too many people to persecute those whom they single out as scapegoats for their own irrational fears, lifelong prejudices, hostility to strangers and people who are different. Putois becomes such a scapegoat for the citizens of the backward town of Saint-Omer. However, for reasons that the reader will soon discover for himself, Putois does not suffer quite so much as the scapegoats in our own midst, hounded by our benighted racists, anti-Semites, or hunters of political bogies. But Putois, too, is more sinned against than sinning. . . .

PUTOIS

"The garden of our childhood," said Monsieur Bergeret, "so small that you could walk across it in twenty strides, was to us a boundless world, filled with pleasures and terrors."

"Lucien, do you remember Putois?" asked Zoé, smiling in her usual way, with lips compressed and her nose over her needlework.

"Indeed, I do!" answered Monsieur Bergeret. "Why, of all the people whom I remember from the time I was a child, Putois remains the clearest in my mind. I have forgotten neither the features of his face nor of his character. He had a pointed head . . ."

"A low forehead," added Mademoiselle Zoé.

Then the brother and sister went on and mechanically listed, each taking a turn and with mock seriousness, the various items of a kind of police description:

"A low forehead."

"Walleyed."

"Shifty-looking."

"A scar on his temple."

"High cheekbones, red and shiny."

"Ragged ears."

"His face devoid of any expression."

"Only by means of his hands, which were constantly in motion, could you guess his thoughts."

"Thin, rather bent, and weak in appearance."

"But really surprisingly strong."

"He could easily bend a five-franc coin between his forefinger and thumb."

"He had an enormous thumb."

"He spoke in a drawl."

"His tone was unctuous."

Suddenly Monsieur Bergeret exclaimed:

"Zoé, we have forgotten his 'yellow hair and his scant beard.' Let us start all over again."

Pauline, who had been listening with amazement to this strange conversation, asked her father and her aunt how they happened to learn this bit of prose by heart, and why they spoke it like a litany, taking turns with recitation and response.

Monsieur Bergeret replied gravely:

"Pauline, what you have just heard is indeed a sacred text, I may say that it is the 'liturgy' of the Bergeret family. So it is fitting that it should be transmitted to you, in order that it may not perish with your aunt and me. Your grandfather, my girl, your grandfather Eloi Bergeret, who was not a man to be amused with trifles, set a high value on this 'passage of prose,' mainly because of its origin. He entitled it 'The Anatomy of Putois.' He used to say that in certain respects he preferred the anatomy of Putois to the anatomy of Quaresmeprenant. 'If the description written by Xenomanes,' he said, 'is more erudite and richer in rare and precious terms, the description of Putois is superior to it in the clarity of its details and the transparency of its style.' This was his judgment, for at that time Dr. Ledouble of Tours had not yet expounded chapters thirty, thirty-one, and thirty-two of the fourth book of Rabelais."

"I don't understand a word you're saying," said Pauline.

"That is because you never knew Putois, my child. You must realize that in the childhood of your father and your aunt Zoé there was no more familiar figure than Putois. In the home of your grandfather Bergeret, Putois was a constant subject of conversation. Each one of us, in turn, believed that he had seen him."

"But who was Putois?" asked Pauline.

Instead of replying, her father began to laugh, and Mademoiselle Zoé also laughed, through her closed lips.

Pauline looked from the one to the other. It seemed odd to her that her aunt should laugh so heartily and even odder that she should laugh at the same thing as her brother. The latter was indeed unusual, for the brother and sister did not have similar turns of mind.

"Papa, do tell me who Putois was. Since you want me to know, tell me."

"Putois, my child, was a gardener. As the son of honest plowmen of Artois he established himself as a nurseryman at Saint-Omer. But he did not satisfy his customers and his business did poorly. Whereupon he gave up his nursery and hired himself out to work by the day. Those who employed him were not always glad that they did so."

At these words, Mademoiselle Bergeret, still laughing, remarked:

"Do you remember, Lucien, when our father couldn't find his inkwell on his desk or his pens, sealing wax, and scissors, and how he kept saying 'I suspect Putois has been here.'"

"Indeed, I remember," said Monsieur Bergeret, "that Putois had a bad reputation!"

"Is that all?" asked Pauline.

"No, my child, it is not all. The strange thing about Putois was that we knew him, that he was familiar to us although . . ."

". . . he did not exist," said Zoé.

Monsieur Bergeret looked at her reproachfully. "What a thing to say, Zoé! Why spoil the story? And do you still maintain that Putois did not exist? Can you prove it? Before deciding that Putois did not exist, that Putois never was, did you give adequate thought to the conditions of existence and the various modes of being? Putois did so exist, sister. It is true, however, that his was an extraordinary kind of existence."

"I understand less and less," said Pauline, growing discouraged.

"The truth will soon become clear to you. First you must know that Putois was born not as an infant but at a mature age. I was then still a toddler and your aunt Zoé was already a young lass. We lived in a small house in a suburb of Saint-Omer. There our parents led a quiet and serene life until they were discovered by an old lady of Saint-Omer, Madame Cornouiller, who lived in her manor of Monplaisir, about twenty miles from the town. She happened to be my mother's great-aunt. Taking advantage of the privilege of kinship, she insisted that our father and mother come to dine with her at Monplaisir every Sunday. These visits bored them to death. The old lady said it was right for relatives to enjoy a family dinner on Sundays, and that only common people ignored this custom. Our poor father wept inwardly with boredom at Monplaisir. His sufferings were pitiful to behold. But Madame Cornouiller was oblivious to them. She saw nothing. My mother showed more fortitude. She suffered as much as my father, and perhaps more, but she took it with a smile."

"Women are born to suffer," said Zoé.

"Sister, every creature living in this world is destined to suffer," remonstrated Monsieur Bergeret. "Madame Cornouiller's carriage came to fetch them every Sunday afternoon.

They were obliged to go to Monplasir; it was a duty they absolutely could not avoid. In short, it was an established procedure which only open rebellion could violate. At last my father revolted and swore he would never again accept Madame Cornouiller's invitations. He left to my mother the task of finding decent excuses and sundry reasons for their refusals—a task for which she was the less gifted of the two. Our mother did not know how to deceive."

"Say rather, Lucien, that she did not want to. Had she chosen to do so, she could have told white lies as well as anyone."

"It is true that when she had good reasons she would rather give those than invent bad ones. Do you remember, Zoé, when one day she said at the table, 'Fortunately Zoé has whooping cough, so we shall not have to go to Monplaisir for a long time.'"

"Yes, that did happen," said Zoé.

"You recovered, Zoé. And one day, soon after, Madame Cornouiller came and said to our mother, 'My dear, I am definitely counting on you and your husband to dine at Monplaisir on Sunday.' Our mother, who had been strongly urged by her husband to give Madame Cornouiller a plausible excuse for declining, could, in her extremity, think only of an excuse devoid of any truth:

" 'I am extremely sorry, dear madame, but it will be impossible for us to come. I expect the gardener on Sunday.'

"At these words, Madame Cornouiller glanced through the glass door of our parlor at the overgrown little garden, where the spindle trees and the lilacs looked as if they had and always would escape anyone's pruning shears. 'You are expecting the gardener! What for? To work in your garden?'

"And our mother, having unwittingly rested her eyes on the patch of unmown lawn and the few wild plants, which she had just called a garden, realized with alarm the unlikelihood of her pretext.

" 'That man could just as well come on Monday or Tuesday,' maintained Madame Cornouiller, 'to work in your . . . garden. What's more, either of these days would be preferable. It is wrong to work on Sunday. Is he busy during the week?'

"I have often noticed," reflected Monsieur Bergeret, "that the most absurd and the most preposterous reasons meet with the least resistance; they overwhelm the opponent. Madame Cornouiller insisted less than might have been expected of a person so disinclined to give in. Rising from her armchair, she asked, 'What, my dear, is your gardener's name?'

" 'Putois,' our mother replied without hesitation.

"Putois was given a name. From that moment he existed. Madame Cornouiller left, mumbling, 'Putois! I am sure I know someone by that name. Putois? Putois. Oh, yes, I know him quite well. But I cannot recall . . . Where does he live? He goes out to work by the day, you say? When people want him, they leave word here or there, where he would be working? There, just as I thought—he is a loafer, a tramp . . . a good-for-nothing! Beware of him, my dear.' "

Monsieurs Goubin and Jean Marteau came visiting. Professor Bergeret apprised them of the subject of the conversation:

"We have been talking about the man whom my mother one day caused to come into being as a gardener of Saint-Omer, giving him a name. Henceforth he functioned."

"My dear Professor," said Monsieur Goubin, "would you kindly say that over again?"

"Gladly," said Monsieur Bergeret. "There was no such gardener. That gardener had not existed up to that moment. My mother said, 'I expect the gardener.' At once the creature materialized. And he functioned."

"But Professor," inquired Monsieur Goubin, wiping the

lenses of his glasses, "how could he have functioned if he did not exist?"

"You see, in a certain sense he did exist," replied Monsieur Bergeret.

"Are you implying that he had an imaginary existence?" Monsieur Goubin retorted scornfully.

"And does your question imply that an imaginary existence is no existence at all?" exclaimed the professor. "Tell me, are not mythical figures capable of influencing men? Think of mythology, Monsieur Goubin, and you will realize that it is not the real characters but the imaginary ones who exercise the deepest and the most lasting influence over the minds of men. Everywhere and always, beings who were no more real than Putois have inspired nations with hatred and love, with terror and hope; they have advocated the committing of crimes, received offerings, shaped manners and laws. Monsieur Goubin, I urge you to think of the mythology of the ages. Putois is a mythological character, he belongs among the more obscure, I admit, and is of the humblest variety. The crude satyr who used to sit at the table with our northern peasants was deemed worthy to appear in one of Jordaens' paintings and in a fable of La Fontaine. The shaggy son of Sycorax was brought into the sublime world of Shakespeare. Putois, less fortunate, will be forever scorned by critics and poets. He has no grandeur, strangeness, style, and personality. He was born in minds too rational, among people who knew how to read and write but no longer possessed that beguiling imagination that creates fantasies. I think, gentlemen, that what I have said is enough to disclose to you the essential nature of Putois."

"I understand it," said Monsieur Goubin.

"Yes, Putois existed. I can prove it. Give the matter your best thought, gentlemen, and you will conclude with me that the condition of being need in no way presuppose a physical existence."

The visitors asked Monsieur Bergeret to tell them about Putois.

"It is very kind of you to ask me," said the professor. "Putois was 'born' in the second half of the nineteenth century, at Saint-Omer. It would have been better for him had he been born centuries earlier, in some mythical forest. He would then have been an evil spirit of marvelous cunning."

"May I pour you a cup of tea, Monsieur Goubin?" asked Pauline.

"Was Putois an evil spirit?" inquired Jean Marteau.

"He was evil," replied Monsieur Bergeret, "in a certain way, but he was not *absolutely* evil. He was like those devils who are said to be very wicked but in whom good qualities are discerned on longer acquaintance. And I am inclined to think that injustice had been done to Putois. Madame Cornouiller was prejudiced against him and immediately suspected him of being a loafer, a drunkard, and a thief. Then, concluding that since he was employed by my mother, who was not rich, he was satisfied with low pay, she wondered whether it might not be to her advantage to hire him in preference to her own gardener, who had a better reputation but who also demanded higher compensation for his work. The season for trimming yew trees was approaching. She calculated that if Madame Eloi Bergeret, who was poor, did not pay Putois much, she who was rich would offer him still less, as it is the practice of the rich to pay less than the poor.

"Already Madame Cornouiller visualized her yew trees shaped into hedges, spheres, and pyramids, without much of an outlay. 'I would keep an eye on Putois,' she said to herself, 'and see that he did not loaf or rob me. I would risk nothing and profit by much. These tramps sometimes work more diligently than upright workmen.' She decided to try him out and said to my mother, 'My dear, send Putois to me. I shall give him work at Monplaisir.' My mother promised. She would gladly have done it. But it was indeed impossible. Madame Cornouiller expected Putois at Monplaisir but she expected him in vain. She was a persistent person, and was determined to carry out her plan.

"When she saw my mother again, she complained of having heard nothing from Putois. 'Did you tell him, my darling, that I was expecting him?'

"'Yes,' said my mother, 'but he is very strange, very unpredictable . . .'

"'Oh, how well I know that sort! I know your Putois through and through. But there is no workman mad enough to refuse to come to work at Monplaisir. My house is well known, I should think. Putois better come for my orders, and without further delay, my dear. Just tell me where he lives; I shall go and find him myself.'

"My mother replied that she didn't know where Putois lived, that he was not known to have an address, that he was without house or home. 'I have not seen him again, Madame. I think he is hiding out somewhere.' She couldn't have put it more truthfully. Yet Madame Cornouiller did not listen to her without mistrust; she suspected my mother of trying to outwit her and keeping Putois out of sight for fear of losing him or causing him to become more demanding in wages. And she judged her to be overselfish. Alas, many judgments universally accepted and sanctioned by history are equally well founded . . ."

"That's quite true," said Pauline.

"What is true?" asked Zoé, who was by now half-asleep.

"That the . . . judgments of history are often . . . false. I remember, Papa, that you said one day, 'It was very naïve of Madame Roland . . . when she was condemned to be guillotined, to appeal to the . . . impartiality . . . of future generations of French people . . . and not to see that . . . that if her contemporaries were wicked . . . those who came after them would be as wicked.'"

"Pauline," inquired Mademoiselle Zoé sternly, "what con-

nection is there between the story of Putois and what you
have just said?"

"Plenty, Aunt."

"I do not see it."

Monsieur Bergeret, who was not averse to digressions, replied to his daughter:

"If all injustices were ultimately righted in this world,
there would be a need for inventing others. Furthermore, is
it possible ever to be absolutely just? And what is justice?
. . . Be that as it may, in the end Madame Cornouiller was
obliged to admit that my mother was not deceiving her and
that Putois was not to be found.

"Nevertheless, she did not give up looking for him. She inquired of all her relatives, friends, neighbors, servants, and
the tradespeople whether they knew Putois. Only two or three
replied that they had never heard of him. Most of these good
people were sure they had seen him.

" 'I've heard that name,' said the cook, 'but I don't remember what the man looks like.'

" 'Putois? I know him very well,' said the road-laborer,
scratching his ear, 'but I couldn't exactly point him out to
you.'

"The most precise information came from Monsieur
Blaise, the town registrar, who stated that he had employed
Putois to chop wood in his yard from the nineteenth to the
twenty-third of October, in the year of the comet.

"One morning, Madame Cornouiller came panting into
my father's study. 'I have just seen Putois. Yes, indeed, I have
just seen him.'

" 'Do you think so?'

" 'I am sure it was he. He was slinking along by Monsieur
Tenchant's wall. Then he turned into the Rue des Abbesses,
walking fast. Then I lost him.'

" 'Was it really he? Is there no doubt in your mind?'

"'There is no doubt about it. He is a man close to fifty, thin, bent, looks like a tramp, wore a dirty shirt.'

"'True, that might fit Putois' description,' said my father.

"'What did I tell you! Besides, I called to him. I cried, *Putois!* and he turned around.'

"'That's the method security police use when they want to make sure of the identity of a lawbreaker they are in search of,' said my father.

"'Did I not tell you it was he? . . . I knew how to track him down, your Putois. I tell you, he is an evil-looking specimen! It was very unwise of you and your wife to employ him. I can read their character in people's faces, and though I only saw his back, I would swear that he is a thief, and maybe even a murderer. He has ragged ears and that is a sure sign.'

"'So, you noticed that his ears were not at all normal?'

"'Nothing escapes me. My dear Monsieur Bergeret, if you do not want to be murdered with your wife and children, do not let Putois into your house again. I advise you to change all your locks.'

"Well, a few days later it happened that Madame Cornouiller had three melons stolen from her kitchen garden. As the thief was not found, she suspected Putois. The police were summoned to Monplaisir, and their report confirmed Madame Cornouiller's suspicions. Gangs of thieves just then roved the countryside, plundering kitchen gardens. But in this case, the robbery seemed to have been committed by a single person, and with consummate skill. There was no sign of other damage and not even a footprint on the soggy ground. The thief could be none other than Putois. This was the opinion of the police sergeant, who had long known about Putois and was making every effort to 'trap that bird.'

"The *Saint-Omer Journal* published an article on Madame Cornouiller's melons, which gave a description of Putois, supplied by various citizens of the town: 'His forehead is low,' said the newspaper, 'he is walleyed; his look is shifty; he has a scar on his temple; he has high cheekbones, red and shiny; his ears are ragged. He is thin, slightly bent, weak in appearance, but really surprisingly strong; he can easily bend a five-franc coin between his forefinger and thumb.'

"'There are good reasons,' declared the newspaper, 'for attributing to him a long series of robberies perpetrated with amazing skill.'

"Putois was the talk of the town. One day the news spread that he had been arrested and jailed. But it was soon discovered that the man whom the police had taken for Putois was a peddler of calendars, named Rigobert. As no charges could be preferred against him, he was released after only fourteen months of precautionary detention. And still Putois could not be found. Madame Cornouiller fell a victim to another robbery, still more daring than the first. Three silver teaspoons were stolen from her sideboard.

"She recognized the hand of Putois in this, had a chain put on her bedroom door, and lay awake nights."

Toward ten o'clock that evening, when Pauline had gone up to her room, Mademoiselle Bergeret said to her brother:

"Don't forget to tell how Putois seduced Madame Cornouiller's cook."

"I was just coming to that," he replied. "To omit it would be to leave out the best part of the story. But all in good time and in the proper sequence. The police made a thorough search for Putois, but in vain. When it was known that he could not be found, everybody tried, out of vanity, to locate him; and the spiteful succeeded. As there were not a few spiteful folk at Saint-Omer and in its vicinity, Putois was spotted at one and the same time in the streets, in the fields, and in the woods. Thus another trait was added to his character. To him was accorded the gift of ubiquity, which so many folk heroes possess. A being who is capable of transporting himself instantly over long distances and who shows

up suddenly in the place where he is least expected, is indeed
alarming. Putois became the terror of Saint-Omer. Madame
Cornouiller, convinced that Putois had robbed her of three
melons and three teaspoons, lived in panic and barricaded
herself at Monplaisir. Bolts, bars, and locks did not reassure
her. Putois was for her a frighteningly uncanny creature who
could pass through closed doors. A household event re-
doubled her alarm. Her cook having been seduced, the time
came when she could no longer conceal her error. But she
obstinately refused to name her seducer."

"Her name was Gudule," said Mademoiselle Zoé.

"Her name was Gudule, and she was thought to be protected against the perils of love by a conspicuous mustache.
A sudden growth of beard protected the maidenhood of that
legendary saintly princess whom the city of Prague venerates.
Her mustache no longer sufficed to protect the virtue of the
no-longer young Gudule. Madame Cornouiller urged Gudule
to identify the man who had taken advantage of her and then
abandoned her to her trouble. Gudule burst into tears but
kept silent. Neither entreaties nor threats had any effect.
Madame Cornouiller made a long and exhaustive investiga-
tion. She discreetly questioned her neighbors, both male and
female, and the tradesmen, the gardener, the road-laborer, the
policeman; nothing put her on the track of the guilty one.
She again tried to obtain a full confession from Gudule:

" 'In your own interest, Gudule, tell me who he is.'

"Gudule remained silent. Suddenly a flash of insight struck
Madame Cornouiller. 'It is Putois!' The cook sobbed and did
not reply. 'You wretched girl! Wretched, wretched girl!'

"And Madame Cornouiller was henceforth convinced that
Putois was the father of her cook's child. Everyone at Saint-
Omer, from the presiding judge of the tribunal to the lamp-
lighter's cur, knew about Gudule and her impending mother-
hood. The news that Putois had seduced Gudule filled the
town with astonishment, admiration, and laughter. Putois was

hailed as a great lady-killer and the lover of eleven thousand
maidens. On such slight grounds was the paternity ascribed to
him of five or six other infants born that year. Considering the joys that awaited them and the delight they brought
to their mothers, these children might just as well not have
come into the world. Yes, many maidens had fallen victim
to Putois' charms.

" 'The monster!' cried the gossips.

"His notoriety spread throughout the town and its environs,
but Putois continued to be associated particularly with our
home, in a thousand subtle ways. He passed by our door, and
it was believed that occasionally he scaled our garden wall.
He was never seen face to face. But we, the children, were
always recognizing his shadow, his voice, his footprints. More
than once, at dusk, we thought we saw his back at the bend of
the road. For my sister and me he had somewhat changed in
character. He remained evil and a malefactor, but at the same
time he became childlike and very simple. He was growing
less and less real, and, if I dare say so, more poetical. He
was about to join the innocent company of children's fantasies.
He was turning into the hobgoblin Croquemitaine, into Father
Fouettard, St. Nicholas' whip-carrying companion, who came
along with him on the saint's day to punish bad little girls
and boys, and into the sandman who shuts the eyes of little
children at night. He was not the elf who visits the stable by
night to knot together the colts' tails. He was not so rustic or
so funny, but as mischievously playful. He drew ink mustaches
on my sister's dolls. We used to hear him as we lay in our
beds before we fell asleep—he would howl on the roofs with
the cats, bark with the dogs, fill the millhopper with groans,
mimic the street songs of the drunkards returning late to their
homes.

"What rendered Putois present and familiar to us, what
intrigued us about him was that his image was associated
with all the objects that surrounded us. Zoé's dolls, my school

notebooks, the pages of which he had so often crumpled and
scrawled upon, the garden wall over which we had seen his
red eyes gleam in the dark, the blue earthenware pot which
one winter night he had split, unless it had been the frost. The
trees, the street benches—everything reminded us of Putois,
our Putois, the children's Putois, a being local and mythical.
In charm and in magic, he fell far short of the most coarse
woodland satyr, of the most uncouth faun. Still, to us he was
a demigod.

"Our father saw Putois quite differently. For him Putois'
character was symbolical and had a philosophical connotation.
Our father had a great pity for humanity. He did not think
men very reasonable. Their misdeeds, when they were not
cruel, amused him and made him laugh. The general belief in
Putois' existence interested him as an example and summary
of all the beliefs of unreasonable humanity. Given to the use
of irony and sarcasm, our father spoke of Putois as if he
were a real person. At times he would be so persistent in this,
and he would describe each circumstance with such exactness,
that our mother would be quite disconcerted and say to him,
'Anyone would think that you are serious, my dear, and yet
you know very well . . .' He replied gravely, 'The whole of
Saint-Omer believes in the existence of Putois. Would I be a
good citizen if I denied it? One must think twice before denying an article of common faith.'

"Only a thoroughly honest mind could have such scruples.
At heart my father was a follower of the philosopher Gas-
sendi—he compromised between his personal views and those
of the public, believing with the Saint-Omerites that Putois
existed, but not believing his direct involvement in the theft
of melons and the seduction of cooks. He professed his faith
in the existence of Putois in order to remain a good citizen
of his town, but he dispensed with Putois when explaining the
events which occurred in Saint-Omer. Thus, in this case as
in all others, he was a gentleman and a good soul.

"As for our mother, she blamed herself a little for the birth of Putois, and not without reason. For in reality Putois came into being as a result of our mother's fib, as the savage Caliban in *The Tempest* was born of a poet's invention. The two falsehoods were, of course, not of equal gravity, and my mother was less to blame than Shakespeare. Yet she was frightened and distressed to see so insignificant a lie grow so out of proportion, and to witness such a minor deception meet with so prodigious a success, spreading throughout a whole town and threatening to spread throughout the world.

"One day she grew pale, believing that she was about to see her fib loom before her. On that day, one of the maids, who was new to the house and the town, came to tell her that a man was asking to see her. He had to speak to madame, he said.

" 'What kind of a man is he?' our mother asked.

" 'A man in a work shirt. He looks like a farmhand.'

" 'Did he give his name?'

" 'Yes, madame, Putois.'

" 'And he is here?'

" 'Yes, madame.'

" 'What does he want?'

" 'He didn't tell me. He will only tell madame.'

" 'Go and ask him.'

"When the servant returned to the kitchen, Putois was no longer there. This encounter of the new servant with Putois was never explained. But I think that from that day my mother began to believe that Putois might possibly exist, and that perhaps she had not lied after all."

PIERRE AND LUCE

Romain Rolland

The selection that follows this commentary consists of the first three chapters from the short war novel, *Pierre and Luce,* by Romain Rolland. Luckily, the excerpt is sufficiently self-contained to justify its inclusion in this volume of short works. Rolland did not publish short stories.

In the tradition of French letters, Romain Rolland (1866–1944) excelled in several literary forms. He was a novelist, playwright, biographer, and essayist. His masterpiece, *Jean Christophe,* generally regarded as the first major twentieth-century French novel, received world-wide recognition. It won Rolland the Nobel Prize in Literature, in 1915. This remarkable study of a young musical genius striving to realize his creative powers and to retain his spiritual integrity in a decadent Europe, captivated a whole generation of youthful readers. The author's exceptional gift for the deep understanding of both the raptures and the anguish of adolescence also lends point and poignancy to the novel *Pierre and Luce,* a story of first love in the atmosphere of the horrifying realities of France at the end of World War I. The duration of the story is from the evening of January 30 to Good Friday, May 29, in 1918. The author finished writing the story in August of the same year. It is very likely based on an actual occurrence. The two main characters are Parisians.

Roland's impassioned stand against war won him friends and followers throughout the world, but it also brought bitter attacks by his overnationalistic countrymen, including some leading French intellectuals. He felt alone, deserted. The Nobel award was given to him by the Swedish Academy at the height of this persecution and when Rolland was in exile. In fact, it was in Switzerland that *Pierre and Luce* was first published. Subsequently, when the patriotic fervors of his fellow Frenchmen had cooled, the book was published in France.

"I do not regard as heroes," wrote Rolland, "those who have triumphed through force or even through brain power. I regard as heroes those alone who are great of heart." With this criterion as a measure of man, Romain Rolland's uncompromising and courageous stand for peace and brotherhood and his compassion for the suffering of his fellow men mark him as an author-*hero* of the first rank.

PIERRE AND LUCE

Pierre plunged into the subway car. A rough and pushing crowd. He stood near the door, boxed in by the human bodies, unable to avoid sharing the heavy breath that came from their mouths. He stared unseeing into the black and echoing vaults over which the gleaming lights of the train flashed. And his mind was sunk in like shadows, with flashes of thought darting therein, hard and ominous. Stifling in the raised collar of his overcoat, his arms jammed against his sides, his lips compressed, his perspiring forehead momentarily cooled by the current of air from the opened doors, he tried not to see, not to breathe, not to think, not to exist. The heart of this boy of eighteen was filled with dull despair.

Above his head, above the shadows of the vaults and the rat-maze through which the iron monster rumbled, swarming with human ants, was—Paris, the snow, the cold January darkness, the nightmare of life and death—the war.

The war. It was four years ago that it had come, to stay. It had weighed heavily on his adolescence. It had caught him in that crucial period when the growing boy, in the turmoil of his awakening sensibilities, discovers with a shock the bestial, blind, crushing forces whose prey he is about to become, and this without even having asked to be born. If he is by nature sensitive, tender of heart, not especially strong in body, as Pierre was, he experiences a disgust, a horror—which he does not confide in others—for all the brutalities, the nastiness, the absurdities of a fecund yet devouring humanity, the breeding sow who consumes her litter.

Every youth from sixteen to eighteen is a bit of a Hamlet. Do not ask him to understand war. (It is simple for you, jaded men!) He has all he can do to understand life, and to forgive it. Normally, he hides in his daydreams and with his preoccupations until such time as the creature becomes used to evolving and has achieved his agonizing passage from larva to winged being. What a need he has for peace and meditation during these April days, so troubled by maturing life. But they come for him in his retreat, drag him from the sheltering shade when he is still so tender in his new skin, and toss him into the raw air and into the mass of hardened human species whose ways he has to adopt on the spot, without understanding them. And without understanding he is expected to pay the penalty for their follies and their hatreds.

Pierre had been called up for military service with others of his class, schoolboys of eighteen. Within six months his country would be needing his flesh. The war had claimed him. Six months of breathing space. Six months! If he could only stop thinking between now and then! If he could only rest in his burrow and not see the cruel daylight.

He withdrew deeper into the shadows, together with the hurtling train, and closed his eyes.

When he opened them again, not far from where he was and separated from him by two other passengers stood a young girl. She had just entered. All he saw of her at first was a delicate profile under the shadow of her hat, a single blond curl on her somewhat wan cheek, a highlight sketching her smooth cheekbone, the fine line of her nose, and her half-parted lips still quivering slightly from running to catch the train. Past the threshold of his eyes into his heart she entered, all of her. And his eyes closed to hold her. He now no longer heard the noises from without. Silence. Peace. She was within him.

The girl did not look at him. She did not yet know that he existed. Yet she was within him. He held her image in his arms, speechless, not daring even to breathe for fear that his breath would graze her loveliness.

At the next station, a stampede. People hurled themselves noisily into the already packed car. Pierre was shoved and pushed farther in by the human wave. And above the subway tunnel, up there in the city, the dull sound of explosions. The train began to pull out. At that moment a man, frantic with pain, covering his face with his hands, came down the subway stairs, staggered, and rolled to the bottom. There was just enough time to catch sight of the blood trickling through his fingers. . . . Then the tunnel and the darkness again. In the train frightened outcries, "The Gothas are bombing again!" During the shared emotion that fused the closely packed bodies, his hand grasped the hand that had just touched him. He raised his eyes and saw it was the girl.

She did not take her hand away. At the pressure of his fingers hers responded with the same feeling, drew together slightly, then relaxed, soft and burning, and still. The two remained thus in the sheltering darkness, their hands like two birds in a nest; and their heart's blood flowed in a single course through the warmth of their palms. They did not speak. They did not move. His mouth almost touched the lock on her cheek and the tip of her ear. She did not look at him. Two stations later she freed her hand—he made no attempt to restrain her—and slipped past the other passengers, leaving the train without having looked at him.

When she had vanished, it occurred to him to follow. . . .
Too late. The train was in motion. At the next stop he ran
up to the street. He found himself in the night's cold, amid
the invisible flurries of the snow, and in the terrified city,
abashed by its terror. High above it circled the birds of war.
Yet he was aware of nothing save the one within him, and he
reached home still holding the hand of the unknown girl.

Pierre Aubier lived with his parents near Place de Cluny.
His father was a judge. His brother, six years older than he,
had enlisted at the beginning of the war. They were a sound,
middle-class family, typically French. They were decent folk,
affectionate and humane, who never dared think for themselves, very likely never imagining that such a thing could be
done. Deeply honest and with a high-minded awareness of
the duties of his office, Judge Aubier would have indignantly
rejected as a supreme insult any insinuation that his verdicts
could be dictated by considerations other than justice and the
voice of his own conscience. But the voice of his conscience
had never spoken (let us better say, never whispered) against
the government. It was the bureaucratic conscience of a
born civil servant. It thought in terms of the role of the State
—diverse but infallible. The established powers were invested
by him with sacred truth. He sincerely admired those souls
of iron, the famously inflexible judges of the past; and he
probably, in secret, regarded himself as one of their de-
scendants. He was a very small model of Michel de L'Hospital, molded by a century of judicial servitude to the government.

As for Madame Aubier, she was as good a Christian as her
husband was a government servant. Just as sincerely and
honestly as he had made himself a docile tool of the powers
that be, against any form of liberty which was not officially
approved, so did she mingle her prayers, in utter purity of
heart, with the homicidal vows then made about the war in

every country of Europe by priests, ministers, rabbis, and
Eastern clergymen, as well as by the press and the conventional thinkers. And both of them, father and mother, loved
their children and felt for them, like all good French people,
nothing but deep and genuine affection. For their children
they would have sacrificed everything. Yet, in order to do as
others did, they would sacrifice them without hesitation. And
to whom? To the unknown god. In every age Abraham has
led Isaac to the pyre. And his glorified madness still remains
an example for misguided humanity.

In this family, as often is the case, the affection was great
but intimacy nil. How could they share their thoughts freely
with one another when each avoided probing into his own
mind? No matter how one felt, certain dogmas simply had to
be accepted. And however troublesome are the dogmas kept
within discreet limits—such as the religious tenets having to
do with the hereafter—how much more so are the secular
ones! Just try to ignore the dogma of "My country right or
wrong!" The new religion, of nationalism, has reverted to the
eye-for-an-eye of the Old Testament. This new religion is
not content with giving lip service and with naïve rituals,
wholesome yet ridiculous, like confession, meatless Fridays,
Sunday rest, which once upon a time absorbed the energies
of our ecclesiastic philosophers—long ago, when our people
were free, under the kings. This new religion demands all
and is not satisfied with anything less—it wants the whole
of man, his body, his blood, his very life, and his thinking
mind. Above all does it want his blood. Never since the time
of the Aztecs of Mexico has there been a divinity so glutted
with blood. It would be profoundly unjust to say that the new
believers did not suffer from their religion. They suffered,
but they went on believing. Oh, my poor fellow men, for
whom suffering itself is proof of the divine! . . . Monsieur
and Madame Aubier suffered like the rest and, like the rest,
worshipped. But you could not expect in a youth such an

abnegation of the heart, of reason, and of common sense. Pierre wanted at least to understand what it was that oppressed him. What a lot of questions burned within him which he could not voice. For his very first words would have been, "But what if I don't believe as you do!" A blasphemy to start with. No, he could not speak out. They would have looked at him with a stupefying fear, with indignation, with grief, and shame.

And because he was at that impressionable age when the soul, with a skin too tender, shrinks from the least evil breeze coming from the world outside, but under its stealthy fingers tremblingly takes shape, he, himself, felt beforehand depressed and ashamed. Oh, how they all believed!—but did all of them really believe? . . . And how did they arrive at this creed? He dared not ask. The non-believer, alone among all those who worship, is like a person lacking some organ, superfluous perhaps, but an organ which all the others have; so, blushing, he keeps his soul's nudity out of sight.

The only one who had been able to understand the boy's anguish was his older brother. Pierre had admired Philippe with the adulation that the young often have—but jealously conceal—for an older brother or sister, or an older acquaintance. It is sometimes only the vision of an hour, soon to vanish, but it represents in the eyes of the young the dream of what they would like to be and of what they would like to love —innocent and disturbing ardors of the future. The older brother was aware of this naïve homage and was flattered by it. It was not so long ago that he had tried to read the youngster's heart and to explain things to him with moderation. For, although more robust, he was, like Pierre, made of that fine clay which, in the case of the better kind of men, retains a little of the woman and does not blush to admit it. But the war had come and torn him from his preoccupations, from his studies of the sciences, from the dreams of a twenty-year-old, and from his intimacy with his younger brother.

Philippe had abandoned everything in the intoxicated idealism at the war's beginning, launching out, like a big crazy bird, into the void, with the heroic and absurd illusion that its beak and talons would put an end to the war and restore to the world the reign of peace. Twice or three times afterward the big bird returned to the nest; but, alas, each time with a little less plumage. He returned without many of his ideals, but he felt too mortified to admit it. He was ashamed even to have had them. How stupid not to have seen life as it is. He was determined now to strip it of its enchantments, and no matter how it revealed itself in wartime, to accept it stoically. And it was not only himself that he punished. A perverse suffering prodded him to destroy those ideals in the heart of the young brother, where he knew they persisted. On his first return, when Pierre had eagerly welcomed him, his walled-in soul so tremulous, he was at once frozen by the greeting the older brother gave him. Philippe was affectionate, as always, but with a harsh irony in his tone. Pierre had to suppress the questions that he wanted to ask. The older brother had seen them coming and with a word or a look brushed them aside. After two or three hesitant attempts Pierre withdrew with an aching heart. He no longer recognized his brother. Philippe recognized Pierre only too well. He saw in him what he himself had been not long ago and what he could never again be. And he made him pay for it. Afterward he was sorry, without showing it, but he soon did it again. Both of them were unhappy. And through a misunderstanding only too common, their suffering, so related, which should have brought them closer, only estranged them. The sole difference between them was that the older brother knew of the common reason for their despondency, whereas Pierre thought himself alone with it, with no one to whom he could turn.

Why then did he not share his despair with those of his own age, his schoolmates? It would seem that these young people ought to have been drawn to one another and to have mutually supported each other. But there was none of this. A dismaying fatality held them paradoxically apart, scattered in small groups. And even within these tiny groups each was distant and reserved. The simpler souls had blindly plunged headlong into the war's current. The largest number had turned aside, feeling no connection with the generations that preceded them; the young did not in any way share their passions, their hopes, or their hatreds. They observed their frenetic actions like abstemious men watching those who had become drunk. But how could they combat the adults? Many had launched little magazines, whose brief lives were snuffed out after the first issues for want of air—censorship had created a vacuum; the best thought of France was under a pneumatic bell. The most distinguished among the students, too restrained to rebel and too proud to complain, resigned themselves to being delivered to the knife of war. While they waited their turn at the slaughterhouse, they stood aside and judged in silence, each one for himself, with some contempt and a great deal of mockery. Their disdainful reaction against the mentality of the herd isolated them in a kind of intellectual and artistic snobbishness. They made an ideal of sensuality, in which the stalked and hunted self justified its stand against human fellowship. Ludicruous fellowship, which showed itself to these young people only in the guise of murder undertaken in common! Their precocious experience with the war had tarnished their illusions—they had seen how little those illusions meant to their elders. Their confidence was shaken in those of their own age as well as in man in general. Besides, it was not safe to confide in others at such a time. They heard daily of some betrayal of expressed opposition or of intimate conversations by some patriotic stool pigeon, whose zeal the powers-that-be honored

and encouraged. Therefore these young people, through dis-
couragement, through disdain, through cautiousness, through
a bitter sense of their spiritual isolation, revealed themselves
little to each other.

Pierre could not find among them the bosom friend, the
Horatio whom young Hamlets of eighteen seek. Although he
had a horror of alienating himself from public opinion, he
felt the need to freely come close to kindred spirits. He was
too sensitive to be able to stand alone. He thought his was a
universal suffering. He was crushed by all the pain on earth,
of which he had an exaggerated idea—for if humanity in
general puts up with it, despite everything, it is because it has
a tougher hide than the fragile new skin of youth. But what
he did not exaggerate to himself, and what oppressed him
even more than the suffering of the world, was the im-
becility of it all.

It is nothing to suffer, it is nothing to die, as long as one
sees a reason for it. Sacrifice may be a good thing when one
understands why it is made. But what sense does the world
and its anguish make to a youth? If he is sincere and sane,
how can he interest himself in the gory squabbles of nations
poised head to head like stupid rams on the edge of an abyss
in which they are both going to wind up? The road was wide
enough for all. Why then this mania for self-destruction? Why
the pride of nations, the rapacity of States, the people who
allow themselves to be taught to kill as a duty? Why the
slaughter of human beings everywhere? Why the warfare and
why the sorrow? Why death? Why life? Why? Why? . . .

That evening, when Pierre returned home the "why" had
become silent.

Yet nothing had changed. There he was—in his room lit-
tered with papers and books. Around him the familiar sounds.
In the street, the bugle announcing the end of an air alert. On
the house stairs the chattering of the tenants coming up from
the shelter. On the floor above, the compulsive pacing of the

elderly neighbor who for months had been waiting for his
soldier son, lost without trace. But here in his own room, there
no longer lurked the anxieties that had lain in ambush for
him.

It happens at times that an unfinished musical chord sounds
harsh; it is disturbing up to the moment when a note joins
it, achieving a fusion of the separate or alien elements, like
guests, who do not know one another, waiting to be introduced. Once the ice is broken, there is an outpouring of
harmony among them. A warm and furtive contact of hands
had been the cause of this emotional chemistry. Pierre was
not conscious of what created the change within him; he
did not think of analyzing it. But he felt that the pall of re-
pugnance of things had unexpectedly lifted. It was like after
having had a shooting pain in the head for hours you suddenly
notice that the pain has disappeared. How did it vanish? There
is still a slight tension at the temples to remind you of it.
Pierre suspected that, under a temporary reprieve, there would
be the return to a much more distressing anguish. He had already experienced the respite afforded by the arts. . . .

When our eyes behold the lovely proportions of lines and
colors, or when into our sensual ears enter the magic cords
that flow and merge with the harmony of the laws of num-
bers, we attain peace, joy fills our being. Yet it is a radiance
that comes from outside us, as from a sun whose distant rays
hold us suspended, fascinated, uplifted above our existence.
The mood lasts only for a moment. Then we fall again. For
art brings always but a fleeting forgetfulness of reality. Pierre
was fearful, anticipating the same deception. But this time
the radiance came from within. Nothing that was part of his
life was forgotten. But now there was a harmony. In his
reminiscences, in his new thoughts. The radiance reached out
even to the objects in his room, animating them and restoring
to them an importance that they had lost.

For months now his intellectual growth had been stunted,

the way the further growth of a blossoming young tree is blighted by untimely frost. He was not one of those practical students who took advantage of the opportunities extended by the university to those about to be drafted—opportunities to hastily grab a degree from under the suddenly indulgent eyes of the examiners. Nor was he one to experience the despairing hunger of the youth who sees death approaching and so takes double mouthfuls, gulping down knowledge that he would never have a chance to verify in life. The constant feeling of the emptiness at the core of things, emptiness that everywhere lay hidden beneath the cruel and absurd ways of the world—this it was that broke Pierre's spirit. He would lose himself in a book, in an idea—then he would stop, discouraged. Where would this lead? What was the use of learning? What was the point of acquiring treasure since inevitably everything would be lost, everything would be left behind, and nothing belonged to him? In order that effort, that learning have any sense, it was necessary that life should have some. This sense no effort of his mind, no appeal from his heart had been able to create for him. And yet, all of itself, it had suddenly reappeared. . . . Life now made sense. . . .

How come? Seeking to find the source of this inner radiance, he saw again the girl's parted lips, which he burned to touch with his. . . .

THE REFORMATORY

Roger Martin du Gard

ROGER MARTIN DU GARD won great acclaim with his cycle novel *The World of the Thibaults*. It was for this work that he was awarded the Nobel Prize for Literature in 1937. "The Reformatory," is a self-contained excerpt from this novel.

The Thibault family lives in Paris. Oscar Thibault, the father of twenty-four-year-old Antoine, about to become a medical doctor, and fifteen-year-old Jacques, a parochial high school student, is a leading figure in the high circles of Catholic laymen. His sons' mother is dead. Monsieur Thibault is a strict disciplinarian, to the constant dismay of the impressionable and turbulent Jacques, who is at the peak of his rebellious adolescence.

Jacques finds himself in almost constant difficulties not only with his father but also with his overstrict teachers. He treasures his friendship with Daniel, a Protestant boy. Daniel's father had virtually deserted the family. The overprotected and overdisciplined Jacques and the rejected Daniel enjoy a soul-intimacy of such intensity as only two unhappy boys with powerful reserves of unexpressed emotion are capable of. They indulge in outpourings of undying affection and mutual admiration. This they do in an exchange of secret letters which they write to each other in a "gray notebook." The boys' ardent style of writing has been affected by the passionate language of the romantic poetry that is currently popular with students and which they devour, together with other forbidden literature, on the sly. Jacques is a budding poet and artist.

Jacques's priest-teacher suspects him of reading censored books and secretly goes through his desk. He finds what he expected, and more—the gray notebook! He bluntly accuses Jacques of having an abnormal relationship with Daniel. Jacques explodes with blazing indignation at the teacher's snooping and appropriating the letters. He is mortified by the nature of the false accusation. He and Daniel decide to run away. They are apprehended by the police in Marseilles and returned to their families in Paris.

Jacques is immediately committed by his father (who adopts the priest's point of view) to a reformatory, founded by him as one of his many philanthropic projects.

Jacques has been at the reformatory, in virtual solitary confinement, for eight months when his brother Antoine pays him a surprise visit. Antoine has been worrying about his young brother, wondering how this high-strung and willful boy was surviving the atmosphere of the reputedly repressive institution. He visits Jacques, to find out . . .

THE REFORMATORY

As the morning express did not stop at Crouy, Antoine had to get off at Venette, the last station before Compiègne. He left the train in a state of elation. The following week he had to take a difficult examination, but he had been unable to concentrate on reading the medical manuals he had brought with him on the trip. The decisive moment was near. For the past two days he had been picturing so vividly the successful outcome of his crusade that he imagined he had already put an end to Jacques's incarceration. His only concern now was to regain his brother's affection.

He had two kilometers to walk along a cheerful, sunlit road. After weeks of rain, there was at last, for the first time that year, a touch of spring in the cool fragrance of the March morning. Antoine looked with delight at the harrowed fields already turned a tender green, at the wisps of vapor lingering in the clear sky, and the hillsides along the Oise river glittering with light. He experienced a moment of doubt, of hoping that he had been wrong—could this be the

setting for a children's jail, in the midst of such peace and
purity?

He had to cross the entire village of Crouy to reach the
grounds of the reformatory. Then suddenly, as he came
around the last houses, he had a shock. Although he had
never seen it before, he recognized the huge building for
what it was, even from a distance. It stood isolated like a
fresh grave, in the middle of a chalk-white plain beret of all
vegetation and surrounded on all sides by bleak, whitewashed
walls. He saw its endless rows of small barred windows and
the dial clock glaring in the sun. It would indeed have been
taken for a prison were it not for the philanthropic inscription
on the cornice, over the first story, which stood out in bold
gold lettering:

The Oscar Thibault Foundation

Antoine proceeded along the treeless walk leading to the
reformatory. The small windows seemed to be watching the
visitor's approach. He reached the front gate and pulled the
bell cord. The clang broke the Sabbath silence. The wicket
opened. An evil watchdog chained to his kennel barked
viciously. Antoine entered the courtyard with its meager garden—a mere lawn encircled by gravel paths that curved
around to the central part of the building, in front of the main
quarters. He had a feeling of being observed although he could
see no living being except the dog, who, straining at his
chain, continued to bark. There was a small chapel with a
stone cross to the left of the entrance. To the right stood a
low building with the sign "Administration." He turned
toward it. The closed door opened the moment he set foot
on the short flight of steps. The dog was still barking. Antoine
entered. The vestibule with its tile floor, ocher walls, and its
row of new chairs looked like a convent parlor. The room
was overheated. A life-size plaster bust of Monsieur Thibault
took on majestic proportions in the low-ceilinged room and

in contrast to the humble crucifix of black wood on the opposite wall. Antoine paused guardedly. No, he had not been mistaken! The place reeked of prison!

Finally a small window in the wall at the end of the room was opened and an attendant stuck out his head. Antoine threw down his card as well as one of his father's and curtly asked to see the director.

Nearly five minutes passed.

Exasperated by the delay, Antoine was about to start on an inspection of the premises unaccompanied when he heard a light step in the corridor; a very fair-haired and very plump, bespectacled young man dressed in brown flannel pajamas skipped up to him in his Turkish slippers, his face beaming as he held out both hands in greeting.

"Good morning, Doctor. What a nice surprise! Your brother will surely be delighted! I know a great deal about you, for the Founder often speaks of his grown-up son the doctor. Besides, there's a marked family likeness. Yes, indeed," he laughed, "I assure you there is. . . . But do come to my office, please. Oh, yes, forgive me for not introducing myself right away—I am Monsieur Faîsme, the director."

He led Antoine to the director's room, shuffling in his slippers and following close behind with his arms extended, his hands open, as if he feared that Antoine might trip and wanting to be able to catch him before he fell.

He asked Antoine to take a seat and installed himself at his desk.

"Is the Founder in good health?" he asked in a piping voice. "He never gets older! What an extraordinary man! And what a pity he couldn't come with you!"

Antoine cast a mistrustful look around the room and unceremoniously scrutinized the young man's face. His fair-complexioned features had a Chinese cast. His slanted eyes behind the gold-rimmed spectacles perpetually twinkled with joy. Unprepared for so voluble a welcome, and nonplused to find the prison warden in the guise of a smiling young man in pajamas instead of the grim-faced martinet whom he had pictured as a gruff gendarme in civilian clothes—or, at best, a forbidding headmaster—Antoine had difficulty recovering his composure.

"Bless your soul!" Monsieur Faîsme suddenly exclaimed, "it's just occurred to me that you've arrived in the middle of Mass! All our children are in chapel, including your brother. What do we do now?" He looked at his watch. "They'll be there another twenty minutes, perhaps another half hour if there are many communions—and that's possible. The Founder must have told you that we have one of the best confessors, a dynamic young priest with incomparable tact. Since his coming the religious fervor of the Foundation has undergone a transformation. How unfortunate to keep you waiting, but what else can we do?"

Remembering the purpose of his visit, Antoine rose without further ceremony. "Your buildings are empty for the present," he said, fixing his eyes on the little man, "would there be any objection to my going through the establishment? I'm curious to have a close look at it—I heard it discussed so often during my childhood."

"Really?" the director said with surprise. "Nothing could be simpler," he added, but he gave no sign of moving. He sat there, smiling, seemingly lost in thought for the moment. "Oh, you know, the place has nothing interesting to offer. It's nothing more than a small barracks."

Antoine remained on his feet.

"However, it interests me, just the same," he said. And as the director stared at him, his small slotted eyes expressing amused incredulity, Antoine insisted, "I mean what I say."

"Very well, Doctor, in that case I'll be delighted. . . . Give me time to put on a jacket and shoes and I'll be at your disposal."

He vanished. Antoine heard a house bell ring. Then a big

bell in the courtyard sounded five times. "Aha!" he thought,
"that's the warning that the enemy is within the gates!"
He was too keyed up to remain seated. He walked to the
window to look out, but the glass was frosted. "Take it easy
now!" he told himself, "and keep your eyes open. First make
sure, then act," and he added, "That's my way!"

After quite a while Faîsme reappeared.

They went out.

"This is our 'court of honor'" the director jested in a pom-
pous tone and laughed excessively. Presently he ran up to
the watchdog who had started barking again and sent the
animal slinking into its kennel with a brutal kick in the ribs.

"Are you anything of a gardener? But, to be sure, a
doctor is apt to be acquainted with plants, by Jove!" He
halted, beaming, in the middle of the scanty garden. "Please
give me your advice—how would you hide that piece of bare
wall? Would you use ivy? I suppose it would take years,
wouldn't it?"

Ignoring the question, Antoine led the way to the main
building. First they visited the ground floor. Antoine walked
ahead of the director, taking in everything and making a point
of opening every closed door. Nothing escaped his attention.
The upper half of the walls was whitewashed but up to the
height of about six feet they were tarred black. All the
windows, like those in the director's office, had frosted glass,
but here they were also reinforced with bars. Antoine tried
to open one of them but a special key was necessary. Faîsme
produced one from a small side pocket and released the
window. Antoine noticed the dexterity of his short, plump,
yellow fingers. The director's eyes swept the inner court with
a policeman's thoroughness. It was a large rectangular area
of well-trodden and dry mud, without a tree and surrounded
by high walls bristling with fragments of broken glass. It
was deserted.

Faîsme described in detail and with great animation the

purposes which the different rooms served—classrooms and shops for carpentry, metalwork, electricity, and so forth. The rooms were small but clean. In the refectory servants were just finishing wiping off the unpainted wooden tables. An acrid smell rose from the sinks in the corners.

"Each boy goes to the sink after the meal to wash his bowl, mug, and spoon. Needless to say, they don't use knives, not even forks. . . ." Antoine gave him a puzzled look. The director added with a wink, "You know, nothing with a point. . . ."

On the upper floor there were more classrooms, more workshops, and showers that didn't seem used much but of which the director seemed particularly proud. He tripped along jovially from room to room, waving his arms as he chattered away. Pausing, he would mechanically push back a carpenter's bench against the wall, pick up a nail from the floor, turn off a dripping faucet, and generally put each room they entered into shipshape order.

On the second floor were the dormitories. They were of two kinds. Most of them contained ten cots covered with gray blankets and arranged in rows; each was equipped with a kit-rack resembling those in military barracks. In the center of each room was a kind of iron cage of fine-meshed wire netting.

"Do you shut them up in that place?" Antoine asked.

Faîsme raised his arms in a gesture of mock dismay and raillery and laughed. "Certainly not!" he said. "That's where the attendant sleeps. You see, he places his bed right in the middle, at an equal distance from the enclosing mesh walls, that way he can see everything and hear everything that goes on and not take chances of being hit with something. Besides, he has an alarm bell whose wires pass under the floor."

The other dormitories consisted of rows of adjoining stone cells; the wall facing the corridor was barred, like an animal cage in a zoo. The director had stopped on the threshold. He smiled wanly, with a disillusioned, pensive expression, which gave his doll-like face the melancholy of certain representations of Buddha.

"Alas, Doctor," he explained, "here we keep our wild ones. I mean the boys who come to us too late to be significantly rehabilitated—they are not our best specimens. . . . These are the kind that are born vicious—don't you agree? We are obliged to isolate that kind at night, what else can we do!" he concluded with a naïve shrug of the shoulders.

Antoine was too absorbed in what he was seeing to think of all the questions he had meant to ask. He did remember one, however:

"What methods of punishment do you use? I'd like to see your 'dungeons.'"

Faîsme drew back a step, opened his eyes wide, and waved his hands in consternation:

"By Jove! Dungeons! But, Doctor, this isn't Roquette, this isn't a notorious convict prison! No, no, we have no dungeons here. Our regulations forbid them; the Founder would never consent to anything like that!"

Confused, Antoine had to put up with the irony that twinkled in the little narrow eyes whose lashes flickered mockingly behind the spectacles. He was beginning to feel burdened by the role of the suspicious investigator which he had assumed. Besides, he was beginning to wonder in his confusion whether the director might not have guessed the motive which had brought him to Crouy. It was hard to know, so genuine appeared the man's candor, despite the malice that occasionally flashed in the corners of his eyes.

The director stopped laughing, came up to Antoine, and put his hand on his arm:

"You were joking, weren't you? You must know as well as I do the effects of excessive severity—it results in rebellion or what is yet worse, hypocrisy. The Founder spoke some fine words on the subject at the Paris Congress, in the year of the Exposition."

Faîsme had lowered his voice and was looking with an expression of deep understanding at the young man, the look saying that he and Antoine were members of an elite singularly qualified to discuss such educational problems without falling into the errors of the common people. Antoine felt flattered, and his favorable impressions grew stronger.

"I admit that in the courtyard, just as in a military barracks, there's a small structure which the architect had named in his blueprint 'Disciplinary Cells.'"

"Is that so?"

"But we put only supplies of coal and potatoes there. What is the use of dungeons?" he added, "You get so much further with persuasion!"

"Really?"

The director smiled a subtle smile and placed his hand on Antoine's arm, saying, "Let me explain. What I call persuasion, I prefer to tell you at the very start, is depriving the offender of certain foods. Our youngsters are all gluttons. Isn't that only natural at their age? Stale bread, Doctor, has an absolutely incredible persuasive power. But you must know how to use it—it is necessary not to isolate the boy whom we are trying to persuade. So you see how unlikely we are to use the isolation cells! No, it is in a corner of the dining hall that the culprit is made to eat his crust of stale bread and during the noon meal, which is the best meal of the day, with the smell of delicious steaming stew in his nostrils, and all the others relishing it before his eyes. That's the way we do it, and the method never fails. Isn't that to be expected? And at that age they thin down quickly. In two or three weeks, never longer, I have attained results even with the most stubborn ones. Persuasion," he concluded, his eyes round with emphasis, "and never have I had to be severe in any other way—I have never raised my hand against any of the youngsters entrusted to my care."

His face was beaming with pride, with good will. He really seemed to love them, those scamps, even the ones who made his life difficult.

They returned to the downstairs quarters. Faîsme took out his watch.

"Finally let me show you a truly edifying scene. I hope you'll tell the Founder. I'm sure he'll be pleased."

They crossed the garden and entered the chapel. Faîsme sprinkled holy water. Antoine saw the backs of some sixty boys in short garments of unbleached cotton kneeling in strict rows on the stone floor. Four uniformed attendants with wooden faces, mustached and wary, marched up and down keeping their eyes fixed on the worshipers. The priest, attended by two acolytes, was concluding the service.

"Where's Jacques?" Antoine whispered.

The director took a few steps forward, pointed to the gallery underneath which they were standing, and tiptoed back toward Antoine.

"Your brother always sits up there," he said as they were walking outside. "He is alone up there; only the young servant who has been assigned to him is with him. Incidentally, you might tell your father that a new servant, the one we had spoken to him about, was assigned to Jacques about a week ago. The other, the old man whom Jacques had before, was getting a little too old for the job, and we are having him supervise a workroom instead. The young man is from Lorraine, and he's a superb fellow, they don't come any better. He's just completed his military service—was a colonel's orderly—and his references are excellent. It'll be less boring for your brother on his walks, don't you agree? But, good heavens! here I prattle on and the boys are coming out. . . ."

The dog began to bark furiously. Faîsme kicked him, adjusted his glasses, and stationed himself in the center of the big courtyard.

Both sides of the chapel door had been thrown open and, three by three, flanked by the attendants, the boys filed out in step, like soldiers on parade. All were bareheaded. All were wearing rope-soled shoes, which gave their walking the muted step of a band of gymnasts. Their jackets were clean and held in at the waist by leather belts, the buckles of which flashed in the sun. The oldest were seventeen to eighteen, the youngest ten or eleven. Most of the inmates had pale complexions, downcast eyes, and a look of placidity incongruous with their youth. But Antoine, though he scrutinized them with keen attention, didn't observe a single telling glance, not one nasty smile, not even an expression of slyness. Those boys did not look like "holy terrors." Antoine had to admit to himself that neither did they look victimized.

When the small procession had vanished into the building and the sound of muffled footsteps continued on the wooden stairs inside, he turned to Monsieur Faîsme, who was looking at him as if waiting for his comment.

"An excellent turnout," he said.

The little man made no comment but softly rubbed one plump hand against the other, as though soaping them, while his eyes, shining with pride behind his glasses, expressed gratitude.

At last, when the courtyard had been cleared, out onto the sunlit chapel portico came Jacques.

Antoine wondered if it were really he. His brother had changed so much, grown so much taller, that Antoine hardly recognized him. Unlike the others, he was not wearing a uniform but a cotton suit, a felt hat, and an overcoat thrown over his shoulders. He was accompanied by a young man of about twenty, sturdily built and fair-haired. Nor was he in official uniform. They came down the steps. They seemed not to notice Antoine and the director. Jacques was walking slowly, his eyes fixed on the ground, and it wasn't till he came within a few yards of Monsieur Faîsme that, raising his head, he stopped, looked astonished, and quickly removed his hat. His reaction was perfectly natural, but Antoine suspected that his surprise was feigned. Yet, Jacques's face remained composed and, though he was smiling, it didn't express any real pleasure. Antoine went toward him and extended his hand in greeting, but his joy, too, was not fully genuine.

"Here is a happy surprise for you, Jacques," the director exclaimed, "but I'm going to give you a bit of a scolding—you must wear your overcoat properly and buttoned up, for chapel. It is cold up there in the gallery and you might get sick."

Jacques had turned away from his brother as soon as he heard Monsieur Faîsme speak to him, and kept looking attentively at the director's face with a respectful but a noticeably anxious expression, as if seeking to grasp the full meaning that the words of the reprimand implied. And, promptly, without answering, he put his arms through the sleeves of his overcoat.

"How you have grown!" Antoine stammered. He kept staring at his brother with amazement, making a great effort to analyze the startling change that had come over the boy's appearance and demeanor, which lessened the spontaneity of his initial reaction to their meeting.

"Would you like to stay outside for a while—it's such a pleasant day," the director suggested. "Jacques will take you to his room after you two have had a little stroll in the garden."

Antoine hesitated. His eyes were asking his brother "Would you like to?"

Jacques didn't seem to have heard Monsieur Faîsme. Antoine took it to mean that he didn't want to remain there, in full view of the reformatory windows.

"No," Antoine said, "we'd better go to your room, right?"

"Do as you like," the director exclaimed with a smile.
"But first let me show you something else—you simply must
have a look at all our 'boarders.' Come along with us,
Jacques."

They followed Faîsme, who, his arms extended, was laughing like a mischievous schoolboy as he was leading them
toward a shed built against the wall near the entrance to the
courtyard. There were a dozen small rabbit hutches inside.
Evidently, Monsieur Faîsme had a passion for raising small
livestock.

"This litter was born on Monday," he announced raptur-
ously, "and, look, they're opening their eyes already, the
darlings. And here, in this hutch, I keep my buck rabbits.
Just look at this fellow, Doctor, he's a 'hard case,'" the
director joked, sticking his arm into the hutch and pulling
out by the ears a huge silver Champagne who kept kicking
against Faîsme with his hindquarters. He didn't say this
with any malice but with a good-natured laugh. Then Antoine
thought of the dormitory and its 'hutches' with iron bars.

Faîsme presently turned to Antoine, smiled the smile of
the unappreciated, and said, "Good heavens, here I am
chattering away and I can see that you're listening to me
only out of politeness, isn't that true? I'll take you as far as
Jacques's door and leave you. Walk ahead of us, Jacques,
show us the way."

Jacques did as he was told. Antoine overtook him and put
a hand on his shoulder. He was trying his best to conjure up
the image of the puny, nervous, undersized creature, the run-
away he had gone to pick up at Marseilles the year before.

"You're now as tall as I am!"

From the shoulder his hand moved up to the boy's neck,
as frail as the neck of a bird. All his limbs seemed to have
stretched to a point of fragility. His elongated wrists pro-
truded from his sleeves, his trousers reached only to above his

ankles. His walk was stiff and ungainly, yet it had, at the
same time, an altogether new suppleness of youth.

The section reserved for the special inmates was in a wing
of the administration building and could be approached only
through it. Five identical rooms gave onto a corridor painted
a deep yellow. Monsieur Faîsme explained that as Jacques
was the only *special* and the other rooms were unoccupied,
the young man who looked after him slept in one, while the
other three were used as storerooms.

"And here's our 'prisoner's cell,'" the director said, poking
Jacques playfully with his plump finger. Jacques looked at
him dully and drew back to let him enter.

Antoine inspected the room with eager interest. It looked
like a hotel bedroom, unpretentious but well-kept. The wall-
paper had a floral pattern and there was enough light, though
it came only from two fanlights of frosted glass criss-crossed
with wire guards and iron bars. These windows were right
below the high ceiling, nearly ten feet above the floor. The
sunlight did not penetrate, but the room was heated, even
overheated, by the central-heating system of the establishment. The furniture consisted of a pitch-pine wardrobe, two
cane chairs, and a black table on which some books and
dictionaries lay in disarray. The small bed was flat and smooth
as a billiard table, and it had been freshly made up with yet-
unused clean sheets. The washbasin stood on a clean cloth,
and there were several immaculate towels on the towel rack.

His minute inspection of the room finally dispelled Antoine's suspicions about the place. Much that he had seen during the past hour had been the exact opposite of what he
had expected. Jacques was properly segregated from the other
inmates and treated with kindly consideration; the director
was a decent fellow, as unlike the warden of a convict prison
as one could imagine. All that his father, the Founder, had
said was exactly true. Obstinate though he was, Antoine was
forced to retract his suspicions one by one.

He caught Monsieur Faîsme's intent gaze on him.

Turning to Jacques, Antoine said abruptly, "You're really pretty comfortable here, aren't you?"

Jacques said nothing. He was taking off his coat and hat which the servant took from him and hung up.

"Your brother has just commented that you're comfortable here," the director prompted.

Jacques swung around. He had a polite, well-mannered air that his brother had never known him to assume before.

"Yes, Mr. Director, very comfortable."

"Now, now, let's not exaggerate," Faîsme remonstrated with a smile. "It's all really very ordinary and we only make sure that it is kept clean. Anyway, it's Arthur we must compliment," he added, turning to the young man. "Here is a bed made well enough for a general's inspection. . . ."

Arthur's face lit up. Antoine, who was watching him, couldn't help making a friendly gesture toward him. The young man had a round head and smooth features, pale eyes, and there was something loyal and forthright in his grin, in his general expression. He had stayed at the door and was twisting his mustache, which seemed almost colorless against his sun-tanned face.

"So this is the jailer I had imagined in the shadows of a dungeon, with lantern in hand and a bunch of keys," Antoine said to himself, and, laughing at himself, he sauntered over to the table and examined the books cheerfully.

"I see you're studying Salluste—are you making good progress with your Latin?" he asked, a self-mocking smile lingering on his face.

It was Faîsme who answered him. "Perhaps it's wrong to say it in front of him," he began with false hesitance and a blinking of the eyelashes in Jacques's direction, "yet I must admit that his tutor is very pleased with his efforts. We work our eight hours a day," he continued in a more serious tone. Then he went up to the blackboard hanging on the wall and straightened it. "Nevertheless, that doesn't prevent us from going out every day, in any kind of weather—your father insists on this—for a good, long two hours' walk with Arthur. Those two have good legs and I leave them free to vary their itinerary. With old Léon it was different; I think they didn't cover much ground, but instead they used to gather medicinal herbs along the hedgerows. I should tell you that old Léon had been a pharmacist's apprentice in his youth and knows a wealth of things about plants, including their Latin names, imagine that! Jacques must have found it very informative. But I'd rather have them take long hikes in the country—that's a lot better for the health."

Antoine had turned to his brother several times while Faîsme was speaking. Jacques seemed to be listening as in a dream, and now and then made an obvious effort to pay attention. At such moments he looked distressed, his lips parted, and his eyelids quivered.

"Good heavens, here I am babbling on, and it's been such a long time since Jacques has seen his big brother!" the director exclaimed, backing toward the door with his little friendly gesticulations. "Are you returning on the eleven o'clock train?" he asked.

Antoine hadn't thought of it, but Faîsme's tone implied that it was the practical thing to do, and, furthermore, Antoine was tempted not to resist this excuse for an early escape. Despite everything else, the dreariness of the place and Jacques's apathy depressed him. He had been reassured by what he observed. There was nothing else for him to do there.

"Yes," he replied, "unfortunately, I must get back early for the afternoon's follow-up visits to my patients."

"There's hardly any choice, since it is the only other train before evening. So long, then."

The brothers were finally left to themselves. There was a moment of uneasiness.

"Take a seat," Jacques said, seating himself on his bed. But noticing a second chair, he changed his mind and offered it to Antoine, taking the first chair for himself.

None of this had escaped Antoine's attention; his suspicions were aroused immediately, and he asked:

"Do you usually have only one chair?"

"Yes. But today Arthur has lent us his, as he does on the days when the tutor comes."

Antoine did not pursue the matter.

"Well, you are pretty well set up here," he remarked, casting another glance around the room. Then, pointing to the clean sheets and towels, he added, "Do they change the linen often?"

"On Sundays."

Antoine had been speaking in the clipped, cheerful manner that was usual with him, but somehow in this echoing room and in view of Jacques's passivity, it sounded somewhat sarcastic, almost taunting.

"Just think," he said, "I was afraid, I hardly know why, that you weren't being treated right."

Jacques looked at him with surprise, and smiled. Antoine didn't take his eyes off his brother's face.

"Tell me the truth, between ourselves, don't you have anything to complain of?"

"Nothing."

"Wouldn't you like me to get something for you from the director?"

"Like what?"

"How would I know? Come, think about it."

Jacques seemed to ponder, smiled again, and shook his head.

"No. You can see for yourself, everything is all right."

His voice was no less changed than everything else about him. It was a man's voice now, expressive and deep, with a pleasant timbre though rather muffled—a quite unexpected kind of voice coming from a mere adolescent.

Antoine looked at him again. "How you've changed!" he said. "No, I shouldn't even use the word 'changed'—you're no longer the same person, not at all, not in any way."

He didn't take his eyes off Jacques, trying to rediscover the former features in the new face. There was still the same red hair, a little darker now and tending to become brown, but still coarse and growing low on the brow. There was the same narrow, poorly-shaped nose, the same chapped lips, shaded now by a faint fringe of down. The same heavy jaw, but now more massive, and the same protruding ears that seemed to pull at the corners of the mouth, making it wide. Yet none of it any longer resembled the earlier Jacques. "His temperament has changed as well," Antoine thought. "He used to be so unpredictable, and always harassed—and now that expressionless face, dormant . . . so excitable in the past, and now so phlegmatic."

"Stand up for a minute," he said.

Jacques allowed himself to be examined with a complacent smile that did not light up his face in the least. There was a kind of film over the pupils of his eyes.

Antoine felt the boy's arms and legs.

"My, how you've shot up! Do you ever feel weak from this rapid growth?"

Jacques shook his head. Antoine stood facing him, holding him by the wrists. He noticed how pale his skin was, seeded with freckles that looked dark against the pallor, and saw the rings under his eyes.

"It's not very good, your color," he went on, with a touch of seriousness; he frowned and was on the point of saying something more, but fell silent.

Suddenly Jacques's submissive, expressionless face revived the suspicion that he had felt when Jacques first appeared in the courtyard.

"They had warned you that I was waiting for you after Mass, right?" he asked abruptly.

Jacques looked at him, puzzled.

"When you came out of the chapel," Antoine persisted, "did you know that I was here?"

"Of course not. How could I have known?" and Jacques smiled with innocent amazement.

Antoine decided not to pursue the matter, murmuring, "I thought they had. . . . Is smoking allowed here?" he asked, changing the subject.

Jacques looked at him anxiously as Antoine held out his cigarette case to him.

"No, I mustn't," he said. And his face clouded over.

Antoine was at a loss what to say. As sometimes happens when one wants to prolong a conversation with a person who barely responds, Antoine racked his brain to think of questions to ask.

"So, there's really nothing you need? Do you have everything you want?"

"Of course."

"Is your bed comfortable? Do you have enough blankets?"

"Oh, yes, sometimes I'm too warm."

"How about your tutor? Is he nice to you?"

"Very."

"Doesn't it bore you too much to work like this, always by yourself?"

"No."

"What about the evenings?"

"I go to bed after dinner, at eight o'clock."

"And you get up at? . . ."

"At half-past six, when the bell rings."

"Does the confessor come to see you sometimes?"

"Yes."

"Is he nice?"

Jacques turned his veiled eyes on Antoine. He didn't understand the question, and didn't answer it.

"Does the director ever visit you?"

"Yes, often."

"He seems pleasant. Do the boys like him?"

"I don't know. . . . Certainly."

"Do you ever get together with . . . the others?"

"Never."

At each question, Jacques, who kept his eyes averted, gave a light shiver, as if it were a strain for him to jump like this from one subject to another.

"And poetry? Do you still write your verse?" Antoine asked in a lively tone.

"Oh, no."

"Why not?"

Jacques gave a little shake of his head. A placid smile spread over his face and lingered there for a while. He would not have smiled differently had Antoine asked him instead, "Do you still play with a hoop?"

Then, at the end of his resources, Antoine decided to talk about Daniel. Jacques was not prepared for this. His cheeks flushed a little.

"How do you expect me to know what is happening to him?" he said. "We don't get letters here."

"But," Antoine went on, "don't you write to him?"

He kept his eyes fixed on his brother. The boy smiled as before, when Antoine had spoken about poetry. He shrugged away the subject.

"All that is ancient history. Let's not talk about it anymore."

What did he mean by that? If he had answered, "No, I've never written to him," Antoine would have bluntly tried to trip him up and would have done so with pleasure, for Jacques's indifference was beginning to get on his nerves. But Jacques had eluded his question, and with a tone of such sad finality that Antoine didn't have the heart to go on. At the same time he saw Jacques suddenly look intently in the direction of the door, as if fearing that someone was eavesdropping. In his irritation, Antoine was beset with all of his old suspicions. That door had a window in it, no doubt to make it possible to observe from the corridor what was going on in the room, and over the door was a grated peephole without a windowpane, through which what was said inside could be overheard.

"There's someone in the corridor, isn't there?" Antoine asked bluntly, but lowering his voice.

Jacques stared at him as if he had lost his sanity.

"What do you mean? Yes, sometimes people pass my door, but why do you ask? Just now I saw old Léon go by."

There was a knock at the door. Léon came in to be introduced to the Founder's elder son. He sat down unceremoniously on the edge of the table.

"Well, do you find he looks well? Hasn't he shot up since autumn?" the old man said, laughing.

He looked like the typical old-time French soldier with his drooping mustache. His hearty laugh suffused his cheekbones with a web of small red veins that extended to the whites of his eyes and dulled his expression, which usually was fatherly but malicious.

"They've sent me off to the workshops," he said with a resigned shrug of his shoulders. "And me, I'd gotten so used to Master Jacques! Ah, well," he added as he was leaving, "it's no use sulking over things. . . . Give my respects to Monsieur Thibault, if you don't mind. Say they're from old man Léon—he knows me well."

"What a nice fellow!" Antoine exclaimed when Léon had gone.

Presently he tried to resume their talk. "I could deliver a letter to Daniel from you, if you want to send one," he said.

And when Jacques looked at him, uncomprehendingly, he asked, "Wouldn't you like to write him a few words?"

He persisted in trying to get the boy to express some emotion, some remembrance of the past, but in vain. Jacques shook his head, not smiling this time, and answered:

"No, thanks. I've nothing to say to him. All that is ancient history."

Antoine left it at that. He felt exasperated. Besides, it was getting late. He took out his watch.

"Half-past ten. I must leave in five minutes."

Antoine hoped that the boy had merely been put off by his matter-of-fact attitude and that the visit might have given him more pleasure than he chose to reveal.

"Are you glad I came?" he murmured self-consciously.

But Jacques's thoughts seemed far away now; he shuddered a little, as if startled, and answered with a polite smile:

"Yes, of course, very glad, thank you."

"Good, I'll try to come again. Good-by." He was feeling annoyed. He looked once more at his young brother, full in the face. All his perceptiveness was on the alert, and he was suddenly moved with solicitude:

"I think of you often, little brother," he ventured. "I always worry about your being unhappy here." They were near the door now. Antoine grasped his brother's hand. "You'd tell me if you were, wouldn't you?"

Jacques looked embarrassed. He leaned toward Antoine as if he were going to confide something in him. Then he seemed to make a quick decision.

"You ought to give something to Arthur, to the young man. He's so helpful, you know," and seeing Antoine hesitate, Jacques added, "Won't you, please!"

"But," Antoine replied, "mightn't it cause . . . complications?"

"No, not at all. Before you leave, stop and say good-by to him, nicely, and give him a small tip. Please!"

He was almost imploring.

"Of course I will. And you—tell me the truth, you lack nothing here? Answer me . . . you are not unhappy?"

"No, certainly not!" Jacques replied with a touch of ill-humor. Then, lowering his voice, he asked, "How much will you give him?"

"I don't know. What do you suggest?—ten francs, will that do, or do you want me to give him twenty?"

"Oh, yes, twenty!" Jacques seemed delighted and embarrassed at the same time. "Thank you, Antoine," and he grasped affectionately the hand his brother extended to him in parting.

Arthur was walking down the corridor as Antoine left Jacques's room. He accepted the tip casually, but his open, slightly childish face flushed with pleasure. He escorted Antoine to the director's office.

"It's a quarter to eleven," Monsieur Faîsme announced. "You've got all the time you need, but you must start at once."

They crossed the vestibule where Monsieur Thibault's bust reigned supreme, and which Antoine now regarded without irony. He now acknowledged how well-founded was his father's pride in his Foundation, created by himself; and he felt a certain pride in being his father's son.

Monsieur Faîsme accompanied him to the gate, commissioning him to present his respects to the Founder. He never stopped laughing as he spoke, puckering his eyes behind the gold-rimmed spectacles, and affectionately holding Antoine's hand in both of his, which were soft and yielding like a woman's.

The little man remained standing at the road, bareheaded in the sunlight, still laughing and wagging his head as a sign of bonhomie.

"I'm as excitable as a silly shopgirl," Antoine said to himself as he walked to the station. "That place is well-run, and, on the whole, Jacques isn't unhappy."

"And the most stupid thing," he suddenly concluded, "is that I wasted time playing the role of interrogating magistrate instead of having a friendly chat with Jacques." He almost decided that his brother was relieved to see him go. "But it's partly his own fault," he thought with annoyance. "He seemed so unresponsive!" But despite everything, Antoine was sorry that he had not expressed more warmth in his first advances.

Antoine did not have a sweetheart and had been satisfied with casual relationships. But his twenty-four-year-old soul sometimes oppressed him—he would have loved to lavish his compassion on some weaker being to whom he could offer his protection. His affection for Jacques was growing stronger with every step he was now taking away from him. When would he see him again? It wouldn't have taken much to make him turn back.

He walked with his eyes lowered in order to avoid the glare of the sun. When he raised them again, he saw that he had taken the wrong way. Some children showed him a short cut through the fields. He quickened his pace. "What if I miss the train," he mused. "What would I do?" He imagined himself returning to the reformatory. He would spend the day with Jacques. He would tell him of his farfetched fears, and of this trip which he had kept secret from their father. This time he would play the part of a trusted friend, a comrade. He would remind the youngster of the scene in the cab on their return from Marseilles, and how that night he had felt they could become real friends. His desire to miss the train became so strong that he slowed his pace though he couldn't come to a final decision. Suddenly he heard the engine whistle. A plume of smoke rose on his left, above the cluster of trees. Without further thought, he began to run. The station was now in sight. He had his ticket in his pocket. He merely

had to cross the rails, run alongside the train, and jump into
a car. His elbows pressed to his sides, his head thrown back,
his beard brushed by the breeze, he ran, taking deep breaths.

He was proud of his good muscles; he was sure he would
get there in time.

But he had reckoned without the embankment. The stretch
of road to the station sloped and made a sharp turn under the
bridge. He ran faster, making his muscles work hard for him.
When he cleared the bridge the train was already in motion.
He had missed it by about a hundred yards.

Such was his conceit that he would not admit his defeat.
He preferred to think, "I could still catch the caboose if I
wanted to, but that would rob me of the chance to see Jacques
again." He stopped, pleased with his "decision."

Immediately, all that he had tentatively planned took con-
crete form: first he would lunch at the inn, then he would
return to the reformatory to spend the rest of the day with his
brother.

It was not quite one o'clock when Antoine found himself
back at the gate of the Thibault Foundation. Monsieur Faîsme
was just going out. He was so taken aback that for a few
moments he seemed turned into stone, except for his little
eyes blinking behind the glasses. Antoine recounted his mis-
adventure. Only then did the director burst out laughing and
regain his speech.

Antoine offered to take his brother out for a walk for the
afternoon.

"Good heavens," exclaimed the troubled director, "our
rules . . ."

But Antoine spoke with such insistence that he got his way.

"Only I must ask you to please explain the special circumstances to the Founder. . . . I'll go and get Jacques."

"I'm coming with you," Antoine said.

He regretted it. They arrived at an unfortunate moment.

They had scarcely entered the corridor when Antoine came
upon his brother squatting in full view in the toilet, which the
staff had named *les vatères*, that is, water closet. The door
was being held wide open by Arthur, who was smoking his
pipe as he leaned against the doorframe.

Antoine walked quickly to Jacques's room. Monsieur
Faîsme was rubbing his hands and seemed jubilant:

"You see?" he exclaimed. "The boys we look after are
looked after all right—even there!"

Jacques returned to his room. Antoine expected that he
would be embarrassed, but he was buttoning up his clothes
quite calmly and his face expressed nothing, not even surprise at Antoine's return. Monsieur Faîsme was saying that
he would permit Jacques to be out with his brother until six.
Jacques watched his face as if he wanted to make sure that he
understood exactly what the man was saying, but he himself
didn't utter a syllable.

"I really must leave you now, please excuse me," Faîsme
said in his reedy voice. "I must attend a meeting of my Municipal Council. I'm the mayor here!" He roared with laughter, as if he had said something devastatingly funny, and was
gone.

Jacques dressed unhurriedly for the outing. Antoine noticed
with what attentiveness Arthur was handing him his clothes.
He even offered to give his shoes a shine, and Jacques let him.

The room had lost the well-kept appearance that had so
pleasantly impressed Antoine that morning. He tried to ascer-
tain the reason. The luncheon tray was still on the table;
there was a dirty plate, an empty mug, bread crumbs. The
clean linen had diasppeared; a single, stained towel hung on
the rack; under the basin was a piece of worn oilcloth. The
white sheets had been replaced by rough, unbleached, thread-
bare ones. His suspicions were again reawakened. But this
time he refrained from asking any questions.

When the two brothers were on the road, Antoine said

cheerfully, "Where shall we go? Do you know Compiègne?
It is a little more than three kilometers away, if you walk
along the Oise. Is that all right with you?"

Jacques agreed. He seemed determined not to disagree
with Antoine about anything.

Antoine slipped his arm through his younger brother's
and fell into step with him.

"What do you think of the towel trick?" he asked. He
glanced at Jacques and laughed.

"The towel trick?" the boy repeated, not understanding.

"Yes, this morning, while I was being taken around, they
took the trouble to give you clean sheets and nice clean
towels. Unluckily, I turned up again when least expected,
and . . ."

Jacques stopped in his tracks, a faint constrained smile on
his lips. "Say, a person would think you prefer to find fault
with everything that goes on at the Foundation," he said,
his deep voice shaking a little. He fell silent for a while and
continued walking, but a moment later he went on, seeming
to force himself to get the words out, as if it bored him
unbearably to have to dwell on so futile a topic:

"It's really quite a lot simpler than you suppose. The linen
is changed on the first and third Sundays of the month.
Arthur, who's been taking care of me for only the past ten
days, had changed the sheets and towels last Sunday, so he
thought he had to change them again this morning, as it was
Sunday. But they must have told him in the linen room that
he had made a mistake, and they had him take back the clean
linen. I'm not entitled to it before next week." He fell silent
again, gazing at the landscape.

The outing had started badly. Antoine applied himself
at once to turning their conversation to something else, but
he was still annoyed at his clumsiness, and he couldn't assume,
as he had wanted, a simple and cheerful tone. Jacques kept

answering yes or no to Antoine's questions, showing not the slightest interest. Then he spoke up, unexpectedly:

"Please, Antoine, don't mention the business about the linen to the director—it would only get Arthur a scolding for nothing."

"All right."

"Nor to Papa either," Jacques added.

"I won't mention it to a soul, don't worry about it. I've already forgotten it. Now, listen, Jacques," he then said, "I'm going to tell you the truth—would you believe it?— I'd begun to feel, and I don't know why, that everything about this place was bad and that you were miserable here."

Jacques turned a little and examined his brother's face with a grave expression.

"I spent the morning snooping around," Antoine continued. "Finally, I thought that I'd been mistaken. Then I pretended to miss my train. I didn't want to leave without having had a chance to talk with you, do you understand what I mean?"

Jacques said nothing. Did he enjoy the prospect of this talk? Antoine wasn't sure. Fearing that he might make a false step, he also kept silent.

The road sloped steadily toward the shore, forcing them to walk more briskly. They soon came to a bend of the river, which had been converted into a canal. A small iron bridge spanned a lock. Three heavy empty barges, their massive brown hulls almost entirely above the water level, were floating on the almost stagnant stream.

"Would you like to take a trip on a barge?" Antoine asked cheerfully. "It would be fun to go down the river through the morning mist, to glide under the branches of the poplars overhanging the water, to stop at the locks now and then— wouldn't it? And at sunset to sit and smoke a cigarette in the bow, thinking of nothing in particular, dangling your legs in the river. . . . By the way, do you still do some drawing?"

This time Jacques reacted with a very noticeable start, and
Antoine was sure that he blushed.

"Why do you ask?" he said in a faltering voice.

"Oh, for no special reason," Antoine replied, but his curiosity was aroused. "I suppose I asked because you could
make a nice sketch of all this—the barges, the lock, and the
charming little footbridge."

The towpath widened, becoming a road. They came to a
wide arm of the Oise whose swollen waters rolled toward
them.

"There's Compiègne," Antoine said.

He had stopped to survey the view shading his eyes from
the sun with his hand. In the distance, he saw above the green
of the woods several pinnacles grouped around a belfry and
the round tower of a church. He was about to make a comment about the pinnacles and turned toward his brother.
Jacques was likewise holding his hand over his eyes and
seemed to be gazing into the distance, but he noticed the
boy's eyes were fixed on the ground. He was listlessly waiting
for Antoine to continue on their walk. They started to walk
again, neither one speaking.

That Sunday all Compiègne seemed to be out of doors.
Antoine and Jacques became part of the crowd. On the
Mall, young women in light-colored dresses and spruce
cavalrymen mingled with the local families passing and greeting each other.

Jacques felt disoriented and bewildered at the sight of so
many people. "Let's get away from here," he begged.

They left the main thoroughfare and turned into a quiet
and somber little street that rose toward the Palace Square.
When they reached it and came out into the open, the blinding
sunlight made Jacques blink. They stopped and sat down
under a cluster of trees which did not yet offer any shade.

"Listen!" the boy said, putting his hand on his brother's
knee. The bells of Saint-Jacques were being sounded for ves-

pers, and their vibrations seemed to become one with the sunlight. Antoine assumed that the boy was unwittingly responding to the enchantment of that first spring Sunday.

"What are you thinking about?" he asked lightly.

But instead of answering, Jacques rose and began to walk
toward the park.

He was not responding in any way to the splendid day.
He apparently wanted most of all to get away from places
where there were people. The calm that reigned around the
château, along its walled terraces, drew him toward it. Antoine followed, making remarks about whatever he happened
to notice—the greenness of the lawns, the doves settling on
the shoulders of the statues. But Jacques's responses were
always vague.

Jacques suddenly asked, "Have you spoken to him?"

"To whom?"

"Daniel."

"Yes. I ran into him one day in the Latin Quarter. Did
you know that he's now a day student at the Louis-le-Grand
Lycée?"

"Oh?" was all Jacques said. Then he added, with a hard-
ness in his voice that for the first time had a little of the
resentful tone that he often assumed in the past, "You didn't
tell him where I was, did you?"

"He didn't ask me. Why? You don't want him to know?"

"No."

"Why?"

"Because."

"An excellent reason! But I suppose you do have another."

Jacques stared blankly at him. He had not understood that
Antoine was kidding. Withdrawn as ever, he started walking
again. Then, abruptly he asked:

"How about Gise? Does she know?"

"Where you are? No, I don't think so. But with children
you can never be sure of anything." Latching on to a topic of

conversation that Jacques himself had opened up, Antoine continued, "There are days when Gise already looks like a young lady, listening to everything that's said with her big beautiful eyes wide open. Then, on other days, she is still a little girl. Would you believe it, yesterday evening Mademoiselle was looking for her everywhere, and there Gise was, playing with her dolls under the hall table! Imagine, and she's almost eleven! . . ."

They were descending toward the wisteria arbor. Jacques halted at the bottom of the steps, beside a sphinx of mottled pink marble, and began to stroke its smooth forehead gleaming in the sunlight. Was he thinking of Gise, or Mademoiselle? Was he picturing to himself the old hall table with its fringed cloth and the silver platter full of visiting cards? Antoine thought so. He went on blithely:

"Darn it, I don't know where Gise gets all her ideas. Heaven knows, our home isn't much fun for a child! Mademoiselle adores her, but you know how she carries on—she incessantly worries about the child's safety, and forbids her everything—doesn't leave her in peace for a second."

Laughing in gay complicity, Antoine glanced at his younger brother. He felt strongly that these little details of their family's life were like a fraternal treasure with a special meaning for both of them, and that it would remain forever unique and irreplaceable. They were memories of their childhood. But Jacques responded only with a faint, forced smile.

Antoine continued nevertheless. "Meals aren't much fun either. Father doesn't say a word, or else treats Mademoiselle to a rehash of his speeches before the various commissions, or tells her in the minutest details how he spent the day. By the way, his election for the Institute is going very well."

"Oh?" A touch of tenderness softened Jacques's expression. He thought a moment and said, "So much the better!"

"All his friends are helping him," Antoine went on. "The abbé is a power to reckon with—he has connections everywhere. The election is in three weeks." He had abandoned his merry tone and added more gravely, "It isn't that important, a membership in the Institute, but it does mean something, and Father has earned the honor, don't you agree?"

"I should say!" Jacques exclaimed and continued with unexpected spontaneity, "He's really a good man at heart!" He stopped, blushed, and wanted to add something but couldn't make up his mind whether to go on.

"I'm waiting for Father to be comfortably ensconced at the Institute before upsetting the *status quo,*" Antoine said. "I'm really terribly cramped in my little room down the hall. I have no place for any more books or for anything else. Did you know that Gise has been put in your old room? Anyway, I'd like to persuade Father to rent the little apartment on the ground floor, the one where that gay old blade has been living. He's moving out on the fifteenth. There are three rooms, and I could have a real study, where I could receive patients, and even a kind of laboratory that I could fix up in the kitchen."

Suddenly he felt ashamed of dwelling on the freedom he was enjoying and on his personal comfort in the presence of a young person cut off from the world. He also realized that he had just spoken of Jacques's room as if he were never coming back to it. He fell silent. Jacques had returned to his mood of indifference.

"And now," Antoine began, changing the subject, "suppose we go and have a bite to eat, would you like that? You must be hungry."

He had finally given up all hope of regaining the brotherly rapport between Jacques and himself.

They returned to the town. The streets swarmed with people buzzing like beehives. Jacques stopped in front of a confectioner's window, fascinated by a five-tiered cake resplendent with icing and oozing with cream.

"All right, let's go inside," Antoine smiled.

Jacques's hands trembled as he took the plate Antoine
handed him. They had sat down at the far end of the shop, in
front of a pyramid of assorted pastries. The rich smell of
vanilla and pies wafted through a dumbwaiter. Without
speaking, Jacques slumped in his chair, his eyes tense, as if
he were going to cry, and ate ravenously. He stopped after
each pastry, waiting for Antoine to offer him the next one,
which he attacked immediately. Antoine ordered two ports.
Jacques's fingers were still trembling as he lifted his glass. He
touched the wine with his lips; it seemed to burn him, and
he coughed. Antoine drank his slowly, pretending not to pay
attention to his brother. Jacques took courage, drank down
a large mouthful, then another, and drained his glass; the port
felt to him like liquid fire. When Antoine began to refill his
glass, he feigned not to notice it, and made a belated gesture
to stop him.

The sun was setting when they left the shop and the tem-
perature had dropped, but Jacques didn't feel the chill. His
cheeks were burning, and the sense of well-being in his
whole body was so unnatural to him now that it was almost
painful.

"We still have three kilometers to cover," Antoine said.
"We must start back."

Jacques was on the verge of tears. Pushing his fists all the
way down in his pockets and clenching his teeth, he walked
with lowered head. Antoine, watching his brother on the sly,
noticed such a change come over his face that he was
alarmed.

"Did our long walk tire you out?"

Antoine's voice seemed to Jacques to have a new note of
affection. Choking with emotion and unable to utter a word,
he turned a grief-stricken face to his brother, and this time
his eyes were filled with tears.

Astounded, Antoine followed him in silence. After they
had crossed the bridge and left the town behind, and were

again on the towpath, he moved closer to Jacques and took his arm.

"You aren't sorry that you missed your usual walk, are you?" he asked with a smile.

Jacques didn't reply. He was overcome by his brother's concern and affectionate tone, by the taste of freedom that had intoxicated him in the past few hours, by the twilight, go gentle and so sad. His emotions were too much for him and he broke into sobs. Antoine put his arm around his brother, steadying him. He no longer sought to penetrate further into the private shadows of Jacques's life, but he was immensely relieved that at last the wall of apathy, which he had tried to break down since that early morning, finally crumbled.

They were alone on the deserted riverbank, alone with the river's darkening current, under the hazy sky flushed with the last fires of the sinking sun. In front of them a small boat was swaying at the end of its chain, making the dry reeds rustle.

They still had a distance to go. They couldn't stay there much longer, Antoine thought. He wanted to make Jacques raise his head.

"What's wrong, Jacques? What makes you cry?"

The boy pressed closer to him. Antoine tried to recall what had released the torrent of tears.

"Was it thinking about your usual walk that made you cry?"

"Yes," Jacques answered, to say something.

"Why did it?" Antoine persisted. "Where do you usually go on Sundays?"

No answer.

"So you don't like the outings with Arthur?"

"No."

"Why don't you tell them? If you'd rather have Léon, I'm sure it would be easy to arrange it."

"No! No!" Jacques cried with unexpected vehemence. He sat up straight and turned to his brother a face filled with such bitterness that Antoine was dumfounded. Sitting still seemed to have become unbearable to Jacques—he rose and began to hurry down the path, dragging his brother after him. He didn't speak. And Antoine, risking being indiscreet, insisted on getting to the bottom of the trouble:

"You didn't like going out with Léon, either?"

Jacques continued to walk, his eyes wide open, and he was gritting his teeth. But he didn't answer.

"Yet he gives the impression of having behaved decently to you," Antoine said.

No answer. He was afraid Jacques was going to shrink within himself again. He tried to take his arm, but the boy shook it off and hurried on. Antoine followed nonplused and was wondering how to regain Jacques's confidence, when, unexpectedly, he slowed his pace, and said through his tears, without looking at his brother:

"Don't tell, Antoine, don't ever tell this to anyone. I didn't go walking with the old man, hardly ever . . ."

He couldn't go on. Antoine was on the verge of asking a question, but sensed that he'd better not utter a sound at that moment. Soon Jacques began to speak again, in a hesitant and slightly hoarse voice:

"The first days, yes. In fact it was on our walks that he began to . . . tell me . . . things. And he lent me books . . . I didn't know such books existed! And after that he offered to mail letters for me, if I wanted . . . it was then that I wrote to Daniel. I had lied to you, I did write . . . but I didn't have the money for stamps. And then the thing started . . . he had noticed that I could draw a little. So . . . you can guess the rest . . . He told me what I was to draw. In exchange he paid for the stamp on my letter to Daniel. In the evening he showed the drawings to the attendants, and they kept on 'ordering' others, more and more elaborate

ones. . . . From that time old Léon didn't bother to take me
out for walks. Instead of going into the country, he used to
take me around the back of the Foundation to the village.
The children would run after us. We used to go through an
alley to get to the tavern and play cards or whatever else, and
while he was in the tavern, I was kept hidden . . . in a
laundry . . . with an old blanket over me. . . ."

"You mean to tell me that they kept you hidden!"

"Yes, in an empty laundry . . . locked up . . . for two
hours."

"But why?"

"I don't know. I suppose the owners of the tavern were
afraid. One day there was some washing to be dried in there,
so I was kept in a passageway instead. The woman there
said . . . said . . ." He broke into sobs again.

"What did she say?"

"She said, 'You never know with this sort of . . .'" He was
sobbing so uncontrollably that he couldn't go on.

"This sort of . . . ?" Antoine prompted.

". . . 'sex criminal.'" He finally uttered the words and
succumbed to a still worse fit of crying.

Antoine was shaken, but his determination to find out
more was, for the moment, stronger than his pity.

"And what else?" he asked. "Tell me the rest."

"Antoine!" Jacques cried, "swear that you won't tell anyone." He stopped, grabbed his brother's arm, and exclaimed,
"Swear to me that you won't say anything! Swear it! If ever
Father suspected anything like that, he'd . . . Papa loves me,
he is so good, it would make him terribly unhappy. It's not
his fault that he doesn't see things our way." And he pleaded,
"Oh, Antoine, don't leave me now! Don't leave me, Antoine!"

"Of course not, trust me, I'm here . . . I won't say a word,
I'll do anything you want. Only tell me the truth." And
seeing that Jacques couldn't bring himself to speak, he added,
"Did he beat you?"

"Who?"

"Léon."

"Oh, no." Jacques was so surprised at the thought that he couldn't help smiling through his tears.

"They don't beat you there?"

"Oh, no!"

"Is that the truth? No one ever? . . ."

"No, no one."

"Then, what else?"

Silence.

"This new man, Arthur? He's not nice?"

Jacques shook his head.

"What's wrong with him? Does he also go to the tavern?"

"No."

"You go for real walks with him?"

"Yes."

"Well, what has he done? Is he nasty with you?"

Jacques hesitated, then answered, ". . . No."

"Then what is it? You don't like him?"

"No."

"Why?"

". . . Because."

Antoine decided he better not insist on an answer. "But why the devil don't you complain?" he exploded. "Why don't you tell the director about it, whatever it is?"

In despair, Jacques pressed his feverish body against his brother.

"No, no, Antoine, you swore you wouldn't tell anyone about it. You know you swore to me that you wouldn't say a word . . ."

"Yes, yes, I'll do as you say. But what I'm asking is, why didn't you complain about Léon to Monsieur Faîsme?"

Jacques merely shook his head, his teeth tightly clenched.

"Do you suspect that the director knows everything and allows it to go on?" Antoine suggested.

"Oh, no!"

"What do you think of the director?"

"Nothing."

"Do you think he mistreats the other boys?"

"No. Why?"

"Well, he seems nice enough, but now I don't know what to think. Léon, too, looked like a good sort. Have you heard anything against the director?"

"Nothing."

"Are the attendants afraid of him? Old Léon and Arthur, are they afraid of him?"

"Yes, a little."

"Why?"

"I don't know. I suppose because he's the director."

"How about you? When he's with you, have you noticed anything?"

"What things?"

"When he comes to see you, how does he treat you?"

"I don't know."

"So you don't dare to speak freely to him?"

"No."

"If you had told him that Léon went off to the tavern instead of taking you for walks, and that you were kept locked in a laundry, what do you think he'd have done?"

"He'd have fired Léon," Jacques answered; there was terror in his voice.

"Then what prevented you from telling him?"

"That, of course."

Antoine was determined to unravel the web of complicities at all cost.

"Listen, is it that you don't want to tell me what kept you from complaining or is it that you don't know what it was?"

"There are some . . . drawings . . . that they forced me . . . to sign," Jacques murmured, lowering his eyes. He hesitated a moment, then blurted out, "But it's not only that . . . you dare not say anything to Monsieur Faîsme . . . it's never done . . . he's the director, don't you understand?"

His tone was weary but sincere. Antoine didn't insist. He was careful not to jump to hasty conclusions.

"In any case, are you doing well in your studies?"

They could now see the sluice gates. The lamps were being lit inside the barges and their lights showed through the small windows. Jacques kept walking, his eyes fixed on the ground.

Antoine repeated the question, "So, your work isn't progressing well, either?"

Jacques shook his head without looking up.

"But the director told me that your tutor is satisfied with you."

"That's what the tutor told him."

"But why did he tell him that if it wasn't true?"

Jacques seemed to have difficulty in following this line of questioning. "Well, you see," he said in a faltering voice, "he, the tutor, is an old man and he doesn't care whether or not I do the work. He comes here because he's been told to come, that's all. He knows nobody will check on him. He stays for an hour, we chat; he's very chummy with me, tells me about Compiègne, his other students, and so on. He's not a happy man. He's told me about his daughter, who has some stomach sickness and quarrels with his wife—he's remarried and the two women don't get along. And his son, who was a company sergeant major, was demoted because he ran into debt over some woman, a cashier. The two of us put up a show with notebooks, assignments, but we don't really do anything."

He stopped. Antoine didn't know what to say. He felt almost intimidated by this youngster who had already been subjected to such a wide experience of life. Besides, he had nothing more to ask. The boy continued speaking voluntarily, in a low, toneless voice, but in an incoherent flow of phrases; Antoine found it impossible to follow the chaotic outpouring, or to understand what forced the boy to pile confidence upon confidence, after his previous obstinate reserve.

". . . It's like with the wine and water . . . you see, I let them have it. Léon asked me to at the beginning . . . and it's all the same to me. . . . I don't care if I drink plain water . . . but what really gets on my nerves is that they're always prowling around in the corridor, with their soft slippers; you can't hear them. Sometimes this even scares me . . . no, it's not that I'm really frightened . . . it's mainly that I can't do a thing without their seeing and hearing me. . . . I'm always alone, but I'm never really alone . . . do you understand what I'm trying to say? . . . not on my walks, not anywhere or at any time! It's nothing much, I know it, but after a time, you know, you've no idea of the effect it has, makes you feel like throwing up. . . . There are days when I'd like to hide under my bed and cry. No, not just to cry, but cry *without being seen,* do you know what I mean? It's like when you came this morning . . . they told me in the chapel. The director sent someone to check on what I was wearing, and they brought over my coat and hat, because I was bareheaded. Oh, don't think they did it to deceive you, Antoine. Not at all—it's just the custom here. Like on Mondays, the first Monday in the month, when Papa comes for the meeting, they always do things like that, insignificant things, to please him. It's the same with the bed linen . . . it's not that they leave me with dirty linen, no, they change it often enough . . . and when I ask for an extra towel, they always let me have one, but it's the custom, you know, to make things look better when a visitor is expected. . . .

"It's wrong, very wrong of me to tell you all this . . . you'll imagine all kinds of things that aren't so. I assure you, I really have nothing to complain about, that the routine is easygoing; they don't try to make things disagreeable, on the

contrary, but it's just this nothingness, do you understand?
There's nothing to do! . . . . stuck there all day with nothing,
absolutely nothing to do! At the beginning the hours seemed
endless, you have no idea! . . . then one day I broke the
winding spring of my watch, and since that day it's been better, and little by little I've gotten used to it. But I don't
know how to say it—it's as if I've gone to sleep. I don't really
suffer, because it's like being asleep . . . but it's painful just
the same, do you understand how it is?"

He was silent for a moment, then went on in a broken
voice, forcing himself to say it:

"And then, Antoine . . . I can't tell you everything . . .
but you probably know how it is . . . alone like that, you
end up having a lot of ugly thoughts . . . the kind you
shouldn't have . . . especially because . . . For instance,
Leon's stories, you know . . . and those drawings . . . Well,
that sort of thing is a kind of diversion, do you understand
that? I make them during the day and at night my mind
dwells on them. I know I shouldn't let it happen . . . only
being alone like that . . . always alone . . . Oh, it's wrong
to tell you all this, I know I'll be sorry for it. But I'm so
worn out this evening . . . I have no control over myself. . . ."

He sobbed.

They hadn't been making much progress and still had half
the distance to go. It was half-past five. There was still daylight but a drifting mist was rising from the river, shrouding
the countryside in a light vapor.

Antoine supported the stumbling boy, all the time thinking
hard—not of what he must do, his mind was already made
up about that. He had decided that, come what may, he must
rescue the boy. But he was racking his brain for a way to get
his consent. That, he knew, wasn't going to be easy. At his
first words Jacques clung to his arm, sobbing, reminding

him that he'd sworn not to say anything and not to do anything.

"Of course not; I've sworn it! I'll do nothing against your
will. Only listen to me. You can't go on like this—the isolation, the idleness, all that sordidness! . . . How could I have
thought, only this morning, that you were happy!"

"But I am happy!" Everything he had complained about
was instantly blotted out from his mind; he only remembered
the advantages of his seclusion, of the idleness, of the lack
of control, and the freedom from oppression by the family.

"Happy? If you were, it would be a disgrace! Not you,
Jacques, I can't believe that you enjoy rotting away here.
You're degrading yourself, allowing your brain to atrophy.
No, this has been going on too long. I've promised you not
to do anything without your consent; I'll keep my word, don't
worry; but give it careful thought—let's look at the cold facts
together, you and me, like two friends. Aren't we friends
now?"

"Yes."

"Then? What are you afraid of?"

"I don't want to go back to Paris."

"Listen, Jacques, after the picture you've presented to
me of your existence here, life at home couldn't be worse!"

"Yes it could!" he cried.

This bitter outcry reduced Antoine to silence. He was more
baffled than ever. "Damn it!" he kept repeating to himself,
unable to think of a way out. Time passed. He felt as if he
were walking in darkness. Then suddenly the gloom lifted, he
found a solution! In a flash the whole plan took form in his
mind. He laughed with relief.

"Jacques!" he exclaimed. "Listen to me, and don't inter-
rupt! . . . yes, do speak, and give me your answer. If we
were to find ourselves, you and me, alone in the world,
wouldn't you like to come and live with me?"

The boy didn't at first grasp the meaning of Antoine's question.

"Oh, Antoine," he said at last, "what do you mean?—there's Papa . . ."

The figure of the father loomed and cast its shadow over the future. The same thought crossed the minds of both: "How easily everything would be solved if suddenly he . . ." Antoine felt ashamed of this thought, which he saw reflected in his brother's gaze.

"Of course," Jacques said, "if I had lived with you, and with no one else, I'd have become quite different. I'd have worked well . . . I would work hard . . . I would, perhaps, become a poet . . . a real . . ."

Antoine stopped him with a gesture.

"Then listen! If I gave you my word that no one except myself would be involved with you, would you agree to leave this place?"

"Ye . . . es . . ." It was because of his hunger for affection and so as not to offend his brother that he agreed.

"But would you let me help you plan your life, your studies, and keep an eye on you generally, as if you were my son?"

"Yes."

"Good!" Antoine said, then kept silent for a while, to think things out. His desires were always so assertive that he never doubted their feasibility. And, indeed, he had so far always obstinately pursued his chosen goals toward their full realization. He turned to his younger brother and smiled.

"It's not just a dream, Jacques," he said, and his tone was determined, although he continued to smile. "I know what I'm taking on. Yes, within two weeks, do you hear me, within just two weeks . . . trust me. . . . Now you go back to that hole, with courage, as though nothing has changed. Within a fortnight, I swear it, you'll be free!"

And Jacques, without fully understanding what his brother was saying, pressed against him, overcome by a craving for tenderness—he wanted to stay close to him for a long time, without moving, to feel the brotherly warmth of his presence.

"Trust me!" Antoine repeated.

Antoine was feeling reassured and somewhat exalted. He took pleasure in his sense of joyous strength. He compared his life with Jacques's. "Poor fellow, things are always happening to him that would happen to no one else!" he thought. He pitied Jacques, but above all he felt a very keen joy at being Antoine, the stable Antoine, so capable of attaining happiness, of becoming somebody, most likely a great doctor! He wanted to quicken his step, to whistle a gay melody. But Jacques was dragging himself along and seemed spent. Anyhow, they were now in Crouy.

"Trust me," he murmured once more, tightening his pressure on Jacques's arm.

Monsieur Faîsme was smoking a cigar in front of the gate. As soon as he caught sight of the brothers, he came tripping toward them.

"All went well, I hope! How was the walk? I bet you went to have a look at Compiègne." He was laughing and pointing in the direction of the town. "Did you walk along the river? Ah! What pretty scenery! What lovely country, don't you agree? . . . I don't mean to tell you what to do, Doctor, but if you don't want to miss your train again . . ."

"I'm off," Antoine said. He turned to his brother and there was emotion in his voice as he said, *"Au revoir,* I'll see you soon, Jacques!"

Night was falling. Antoine dimly saw Jacques's submissive face, his swollen eyelids, and his gaze riveted to the ground. He repeated:

"Au revoir!"

A CHRISTMAS TALE

François Mauriac

FRANÇOIS MAURIAC (1885–   ), novelist, critic, and journalist, published only one slim volume of short stories, under the title of *Plongées* (Introspections), in 1933. "A Christmas Tale" is one of these *plongées*. It is the author's reminiscence of a religious experience on Christmas Eve, when he was seven. This experience was as important to his existence as an incident on the same occasion proved to be to a school friend of the same age.

Mauriac is closely identified with Roman Catholicism and is regarded as a leading "Catholic novelist." But, far from advocating a simplistic and dogmatic adherence to religious doctrine and ritual to solve modern man's spiritual failings and falterings, he urges a delving into the depths of the subconscious. This Mauriac does with the characters of his novels and stories, with his "dark heroes," men, women, and, occasionally even children, threatened with spiritual breakdown. Jean de Blaye in "A Christmas Tale" is one such "dark hero."

The tone of this story is not notably modern, but the psychological overtones in its characterizations bring it close to our own times.

A CHRISTMAS TALE

A scraggy plane tree, seemingly reaching up for air, stretched over the high walls of the courtyard into which we had just been released. But on that day we had not exploded with our usual shouts at the sound of Monsieur Garouste's whistle. It was the day before Christmas. We had been sentenced to a hike in the suburbs, through the fog and the mud, and we now felt as weary as only seven-year-old boys can feel whose young legs have trudged some fifteen kilometers.

The boarding students were putting on their house slippers. The flock of day students stood facing the gate, waiting for those who would come to deliver them from their daily captivity. I was munching absently and without appetite on a piece of bread, my mind already preoccupied with the mystique of that special evening which would soon excite me, and whose ritual never changed. They would have us wait behind the closed door of the guest room as the candles of the crèche were being lit. Then we would hear Mother call out, "You may come in." We would hurry eagerly into the

room, which for us came to life only on that night. The
tiny flames would draw us toward the little world of shep-
herds and beasts crowded around the Child. A night light
illumining the interior of King Herod's crenelated castle,
atop a mountain made of crumpled wrapping paper, would
give us the illusion that we were present at secret and forbidden festivities. We would kneel and sing the carol of adora-
tion.

> *A stable was his lodging,*
> *A pile of hay his crib,*
> *A stable was his lodging,*
> *How humble for a God!*

The humility of God would touch our hearts. . . . Behind the crèche there would be a gift for each one of us, together with a letter in which God himself had written down
our most grievous sin. As I stood in the courtyard facing the
gate, I already felt the surrounding shadows of that unused
room; no imaginary thief was now there, holding his breath
behind the heavy, dark-flowered drapes drawn across the
alcoves and windows. On the walls of the room, portraits of
the dead listened from the depths of eternity to our feeble
voices. Then, when the night would begin, before falling off
to sleep, each child would take a last peek at his hobnailed
shoes—the largest pair he possessed—which he had chosen
to play a role in the miracle which every Christmas I tried in
vain to surprise; but sleep is a chasm that no child can evade.

Thus I lived through in advance that blessed evening, as I
stood facing the gate through which my nurse would soon
appear. The light was already fading. Although it was not yet
four o'clock, I waited impatiently, hoping that she would arrive early. All of a sudden a racket arose in a corner of the
schoolyard. Many of the children rushed in that direction,
yelling, "Look at the girl! Look at the girl!" The long curls of

little Jean de Blaye doomed him to this persecution. His
locks seemed hideous to us, with our shaved skulls. I was
the only one who admired them, but secretly, mainly because
they reminded me of the curls of little Lord Fauntleroy,
whose story I had loved ever since it appeared in the *Saint-
Nicolas* magazine of 1887. Whenever I was in the mood to
pity myself or to cry, it was enough for me to look at the
picture of the little lord in his mother's arms and to read the
legend underneath: "Yes, she had always been his best, his
most tender friend. . . ." But the other children didn't have
that issue of *Saint-Nicolas;* they didn't know that Jean de
Blaye had a resemblance to Fauntleroy, so they tormented
him; and I, a coward because I felt myself to be so weak
against so many, kept my distance.

On that day, however, I was astonished because the pack
didn't stop with "Look at the girl!" but used other taunting
words as well, words that at first I didn't understand. I went
closer, hugging the wall, afraid to attract the attention of the
leader, the persecutor and sworn enemy of Jean de Blaye.
His name was Campagne. He had been left back twice and
was a head taller than any of us, a veritable giant in our eyes,
endowed with almost supernatural physical strength. The children encircled Jean de Blaye, shouting:

"He believes it! He believes it! He believes it!"

"What does he believe?" I asked one of them.

"He believes that it is little Jesus who comes down the
chimney. . . ."

I didn't understand, and asked: "What of it?" But the other
boy had again begun to howl with the wolves. I moved closer.
Campagne had grabbed little de Blaye by the wrists and had
pushed him against the wall.

"Do you believe it, yes or no?"

"Stop! You're hurting me!"

"Admit it and I'll let you go."

Then little de Blaye proclaimed in a loud, firm voice, like
a martyr confessing his faith:

"Mama told me, and mama never lies."

"Did you hear that!" howled Campagne. "Missy's mother
never lies."

Through our servile laughter, Jean de Blaye repeated:
"Mama does not lie! Mama would not fool me. . . ." At that
moment he saw me and appealed to me:

"Tell them, Frontenac—you know it's true. We were talking about it just a while ago, on the hike."

Campagne turned his cruel cat's eyes on me and I stammered: "I was only fooling him. . . ." Seven years old—an
age of weakness, of cowardice. Monsieur Garouste came up
at that moment and the gang melted away. We went to get
our raincoats and schoolbags.

When we got to the street, Jean de Blaye caught up to me.
The manservant who had come for him was glad to walk
with my nurse.

"You know very well it's true . . . but you were scared of
Campagne. . . . Wasn't that it? Wasn't it because you were
scared?"

I was badly confused. I denied being afraid of Campagne. I
said no, I didn't know whether or not it was true. After all, it
didn't much matter as long as we got the toy we had asked
for. But how did little Jesus know that Jean wanted some lead
soldiers, a box of tools, and I a stable and a farm? . . . Why
did the toys come from the Universal Department Store?

"Who told you that?"

"Last year I saw the labels . . ."

Jean de Blaye kept repeating, "Just the same, since Mama
said so . . ." and I could see that he was upset.

"Listen," I said, "if we really want absolutely not to fall
asleep, all we have to do is relight the candle, take a book,

get settled in an armchair by the fireplace, and we will be sure to be awake when He comes. . . ."

"Mama says that if you don't go to sleep, you keep Him from coming."

The lights of the store windows glittered on the sidewalks which were wet with the evening mist. Temporary booths lined the Concourse des Fossés. The acetylene lamps in the confectionary shop were shining on the pink candies which we longed for, but which were of such poor quality that we were not allowed to buy them.

"We could pretend to be asleep," I said.

"He'd know perfectly well that we were pretending, because He knows everything. . . ."

"But if it is Mother who leaves the gifts and not He, she'll make believe she doesn't notice."

Jean de Blaye insisted, "It'll not be Mama!" We had reached the street corner where we were going to part until the end of the holidays, for Jean was leaving the next day for the country. I begged him to try not to fall asleep; as for myself, I was determined to stay awake. We'd tell each other what we saw. He promised that he'd try. I watched him go. For a few seconds I saw his long girlish curls bobbing on his shoulders; then his little figure vanished in the evening mist.

Our house was near the cathedral. On Christmas Eve the big bell in the Pey-Berland tower would fill the darkness with a thunderous booming. My bed would then become a ship's berth and the sound would hold me, rocking me in its tempest. The flickering night candle peopled the room with familiar phantoms. The curtain windows, the table, my clothes lying in disorder on the armchair no longer surrounded my bed menacingly—I had tamed these beasts. They would guard my sleep like the jungle beasts who watched over the boy Mowgli.

I wasn't going to take a chance of falling asleep that evening. The ringing of the cathedral bell helped keep me awake.

My fingers grabbed the bars of the bedstead, so real seemed the feeling of being delivered up, body and soul, to a beneficent storm. Then Mother opened the door. My eyelids were closed but I recognized the silken sound of her dress. If it was she who placed the toys at my shoes, this would be the moment, I told myself, now, before she left for midnight Mass. I made an effort to breathe like a sleeping child. Mother bent over me and I felt her breath. This proved stronger than all my resolutions. I threw my arms around her neck and pressed against her with a kind of frenzy.

"Oh, you little madman! Oh, you little madman! How do you expect Him to come if you don't go to sleep? Go to sleep, Yves my darling, go to sleep my child. . . ."

"Mother, I want to see Him!"

"He wants to be loved without being seen. . . . You know, don't you, that in the Mass, the moment when He descends to the altar all heads are lowered. . . ."

"Mother, don't be angry, but once I didn't lower my head— I kept looking—I saw Him. . . ."

"What? You saw Him?"

"Yes . . . at least . . . the tip of a white wing. . . ."

"Anyway, this isn't the night to keep your eyes open. You'll see Him best if you are asleep. You'd better not be awake by the time we get back from church!"

She closed the door after her, and I could hear her departing footsteps. I lit the candle and turned toward the fireplace; the last embers were dying. My shoes stood there, between the andirons and at the outside edge of the sooty square covered with cinders and ashes. It was down the chimney and through the trap door that the thunderous sound of the big bell flowed into my room. It filled it with an awesome song which, before reaching me, had rolled above the rooftops and up to the Milky Way where on Christmas Eve thousands of angels and stars mingled. What would have surprised me now would not have been the appearance of the Child in the dark recess of the hearth, but, on the contrary, if nothing had happened. Besides, something was already happening: my two shoes, the space around them still empty, those poor old heavy shoes which were so much a part of my daily life, suddenly took on a strange and unreal aspect, as if they had been placed there almost at a time beyond time, as if a little boy's shoes could suddenly be touched by an illumination cast from an invisible world. So close was the miracle that I blew out the candle in order not to startle the invisible ones on this night of nights.

If time seemed to pass quickly it was no doubt because I was suspended in timelessness. Someone pushed open the door and I closed my eyes. Hearing the silken whisper of the dress, the rustle of paper, I told myself it must be Mother. It was she and it wasn't she; it appeared to me rather that someone else had been transmuted into the form of my mother. During that midnight Mass, which I had not attended and which was beyond my imagination, I knew that Mother and my brothers must have received the little Host and that they had returned to their seats, as I had seen them do so often, with their hands folded in prayer and their eyelids closed so tight that I wondered how they were able to find their way. To be sure, it was Mother. After having lingered at the fireplace, she approached my bed. But He lived in her. I could not think of them separately. The breath which I felt on my hair came from her in whom the spirit of God still dwelt. It was at that moment that I sank into my mother's arms and into sleep.

The first morning back at school I wore the shoes that had been part of the miracle and which were now only a pair of ordinary, hobnailed, schoolboy's shoes, splashing like an ass's hoofs in the schoolyard puddles around the plane tree, as I waited for the eight o'clock bell. I looked in vain for the girlish locks of Jean de Blaye among the mob of children

shouting and chasing each other. I couldn't wait to tell him
the secret I had discovered . . . But, exactly what was the
secret? I tried to imagine the words I would have to use
to make him understand me.

Jean de Blaye's curls were still nowhere to be seen. Was
he home, sick? Maybe it would be a long time before I found
out what he had seen during his night of watching? After entering the classroom my eyes remained fixed on the seat he
usually occupied. A different child was sitting there, a child
without curls. At first I didn't realize that it was he. I would
never have recognized him except by the blue eyes that turned
toward me; and what astonished me the most was his air
of casualness, of ease. He was shorn somewhat less than his
schoolmates. The barber had left his hair long enough, so that
he could part it on the left side.

At the ten o'clock recess, as soon as we were set loose in
the courtyard, I went looking for him and saw him, erect as
a little David in front of big Campagne, as if it had been his
weakness and not his strength that he had lost with his hair.
Campagne was so put off by what had just transpired between
them that he left the field to Jean de Blaye, who coolly sat
down on the steps to put on his roller skates. I watched him
from a distance, undecided, thinking with a certain amount
of sadness that I would never again see the curls of little
Lord Fauntleroy gleam in the sunlight or dance on the shoulders of Jean de Blaye. I finally made up my mind to walk
over to him.

"Well? Did you keep your promise?" I said. "Did you stay
awake?"

He muttered, without raising his head: "Go on, did you
really think I believed all that . . . that I could be so stupid?"
And as I continued, "But, remember? . . . it was only two
weeks ago," he bent a little lower over his skates and assured
me that he had been pretending, that he had been making a

fool of me, adding, "After all, at our age, when we are eight, we are no longer children."

He kept talking without looking at me; I could not see the expression in his eyes, and could no longer hold back the burning question:

"So, tell me—did your mother deceive you?"

He had put one knee on the ground in order to tighten the strap of his skate. Blood rushed to his ears, naked now as the wings of Zephyr. I kept mercilessly insisting:

"Come on, de Blaye, tell me: your mother—did she fool you?"

He straightened up suddenly and looked me in the eye. I can still see that young face, sullen and flushed, his lips tight. He brushed his hand over his head as if he sought the absent curls, and shrugged:

"She'll never fool me again."

I replied almost in spite of myself that our mothers had not lied to us, that it was all true, that I had seen . . . He interrupted me:

"You saw? . . . Is that true? You saw? . . . Well, I saw something too!"

With that he skated away, and to the end of the recess he never stopped skating around the plane tree. I understood that he was avoiding me. From that day we were no longer friends. The next year his family left Bordeaux, and I didn't know what became of him.

It happened only once during my youth in Paris that I didn't spend Christmas Eve in the provinces, with my people. That one time must have been only a few years before the war. I made the rounds of the nightclubs. I have since forgotten their names, but I still remember the consuming homesickness. In the atmosphere of those "dives," the big bell of the Pey-Berland tower of our cathedral must have resounded within me with a greater force than it did, that childhood

evening, over the roofs of my native town. Its overpowering
voice now drowned out the gypsies' violins. It is at such
evocative moments in life that a person feels certain of having betrayed his ideals. My companions for the evening were
not such traitors to themselves. They had no choice to make.
Perhaps some of them had had a childhood like mine, but
they had very likely forgotten it. I believe I was the only one
in that room filled with food odors and the din of insipid
melodies to recapture in my imagination the shadows of that
guest room, the magic of the little island of the crèche. I must
have been the only one there who recalled the ancient carol
about the humility of God. Although I was only in the
prime of my youth, those flickering candles in the past were
now so remote that I seemed to be a thousand years old. I
could feel their glow nevertheless, for I was a poet and in a
poet's heart nothing is ever extinguished. How could I, then,
have brought there, how had I dared to drag there that night
the childhood which had never left me?"

I drank in order to lose awareness of my offense. The more
I drank, the more distant did I feel from my companions.
How their silly merriment annoyed me! I left the table and
walked over to the bar, where the lights were more subdued.
I leaned against it and ordered a whisky. And at the very moment when I was thinking about a little boy named Jean de
Blaye, whom should I see but Jean de Blaye himself. He was
perched on a stool next to me. I was certain it was he. The
same gleaming periwinkle-blue eyes were lighting up the tired
lines of this young man's face. His face was close enough for
me to touch it. I said to him:

"They shouldn't have cut off your curls."

He didn't seem to be surprised, but he asked in a rather
thick voice, "What curls?"

"The ones that were cut off during the Christmas holiday—
when we were seven."

"You're taking me for someone else, of course, but that

doesn't matter . . . I happen not to feel much like myself this evening."

"I know you're de Blaye."

"How do you know my name?"

I let out a sigh—it was he! It was, indeed he! I reached for his hand, to shake it.

"Jean, do you remember that plane tree?"

He laughed. "The plane tree . . . which plane tree? By the way, my name isn't Jean but Philippe. My older brother's name was Jean. Perhaps you're mistaking me for him?"

"What a pity. You must be the younger brother about whom Jean used to speak." How could I have made such a mistake? Philippe's face lacked Jean's vivacity. He said suddenly:

"Those curls . . . yes, those curls of Jean's . . . that reminds me of an incident. . . ."

He told me about it: in his mother's room there had been a chest on which she kept a locked silver casket. Jean had assured Philippe that it contained a treasure. They kept wondering about it, but their mother refused to show them what was in the casket, and she forbade them ever to open it. She and Jean were always bickering, always at odds. "She loved him more than me," said Philippe, "and in the end I became convinced that she had loved no one but him. . . . Nevertheless, something set them against each other—I don't know what. . . . One day Jean forced the lock on the casket . . . the first lock that he had forced, but alas! not the last! The treasure . . . it was, would you believe it, his infant curls. One would have thought they were the hair of a corpse! Jean threw one of his tantrums. . . . You know how he would carry on at such times. He stopped fuming only when he saw his old curls burning in the fireplace. That evening my mother . . . But I don't know why I'm telling you all this. . . ." He returned to his drink. I thought to myself: "He speaks of his brother in the past." Somehow I knew in

advance the answer to the question that I now asked him,
"Is he dead?"

"Last year . . . in a hospital in Saigon. There was a notice
in the paper but they didn't notify us. . . . Who could blame
them, after all those episodes, after the life he had led . . ."

I could have asked, "What kind of a life?" I preferred to
say, "Yes, yes . . . I understand . . ." and I knew that Jean
had perished as a depraved youth, a lost soul.

I remember returning later to my student lodgings on foot.
Lean plane trees hung over the fences, over the muddy sidewalks, their branches bathed in the dawn mist. There were
still many revelers in the streets. I saw my evening's companions hoist a drunken woman into a red cab. Far from the dis-
orders of the evening's festivities, my eyes sought over the
roofs, up in the frozen heights, the angels now wakened by
the big bell of the Pey-Berland tower. There is such a thing as
a lucid state of drunkenness. At the same time that I felt uplifted, not only by the reminiscences of my childhood but by
my childhood itself, alive and vivid within me, I reconstructed
with amazing ease Jean de Blaye's story. I may have been
born a poet, but that night I became a novelist, at least I became aware of that gift, of that power. I walked rapidly,
lightly, carried away by the force of creativity. I conceived
the two poles of his fate: a small boy with girl's hair, whose
soul was ruled by a wild compulsiveness and a powerful passion totally centered on his mother, and then the man, still almost a child, who suffered his last agony on a hospital bed, in
Saigon.

I recreated the schoolboy for whom his mother's word
was sacred. I saw his horror at the moment when he discovered that she was capable of lying; I saw a special meaning in his shorn curls: their demise marked the end of his
filial love. . . . Here ended the prologue to my novel and I
launched into the heart of the theme: that young male and
that mother in confrontation; the scene with the casket be-

came the core of it. Jean de Blaye hated in her who had brought him into the world the determination to perpetuate the infant that he no longer was, to keep him prisoner of his childhood, in order to hold him more relentlessly under her domination. Barely had manhood begun to rise in him, than the struggle against her resolve turned into a tragedy—his first friendship, his first love, the first night when he didn't come home, the demands for money, the clandestine companions, the first serious crime . . .

I arrived at my door. The day had dawned. The bells were announcing the sunrise Mass. Despite my need for sleep, I sat down at my desk at once, in my evening clothes and my boutonniere still in my lapel, and took up a pen and a blank sheet of paper, so anxious was I not to forget the ideas that had come to me! A novelist had just been born, opening his eyes on this sad world.

THE RETURN OF
THE PRODIGAL SON

André Gide

The life of ANDRÉ GIDE (1869–1951), novelist, critic, satirist, moralist, stylist, and short-story writer, extended over a period of eighty-two years. It had an important influence on generations of youth. Gide received the Nobel award in 1947. In his numerous works he was predominantly a dissenter from traditional institutions and thought, that is, a critic of what we now call "the establishment." Reared in an extremely puritanical Protestant family, he liberated himself as a young man from its rigid morality, achieving this with great determination and with as great anguish. Gradually he matured into a twentieth-century questioning Socrates, and, like the Greek philosopher, he was accused by his enemies of wrongly influencing the young, a criticism leveled against most of history's daring thinkers. Despite this violent criticism, Gide continued to believe that his function as a writer was to disturb, to prod his reader to test various ossified common beliefs and codes, to reach for the truth.

A later test of Gide's independence of mind came with the strong movement among French intellectuals, due to the disillusionments of the early years of this century, to seek refuge in Roman Catholicism. Again, as in his youth, he was tormented by the duality in his nature—to believe and to question. This inner struggle became so severe at this period that he was unable to write for a number of years. Then he finally resolved the conflict. He clarified this resolution in the allegorical tale, written with the intensity of a tone poem, "The Return of the Prodigal Son," published in 1907. Now the will and the inspiration to write was restored to him, and Gide continued to produce important literary works for nearly another fifty years.

The allegory must be read with the author's complex symbolism in mind. Basing himself on the parable of the prodigal son, as recounted by Luke in the New Testament, Gide uses the theme as a mirror, flashing it now on the temporal family, now on the established order, now on the church, and in the end on the universal prodigal, the rebel who feels an irresistible urge to liberate himself from the dogmatic restrictions imposed on his freedom by traditional thought, so that he may explore, experience, and experiment, in other words, so that he may choose what is right for *him*.

Approaching the biblical parable with imagination, Gide adds two characters to it: the mother and the younger brother. The prodigal son is the strayer from the "house and the enclosed garden," which are also the church, any church; the father is the parent, any authority, or a limited vision of God; the mother is an indulgent parent, the protective arms of dogma, or the mother church; the elder brother is the conventional, overpractical individual, or the ritualistic church and its traditional clergy. The younger brother is the young seeker, the ever-present *prodigal*.

THE RETURN OF THE PRODIGAL SON

After a long absence, grown weary of his whims and no longer impressed with himself, the prodigal son, from the depth of his poverty that he had sought, thinks of his father's face. He thinks of that fairly large room where his mother used to bend over his bed, the garden watered by a running stream but fully walled in, from which he had always wanted to escape, the practical brother whom he never loved but who still holds in trust that share of his fortune which he, the prodigal, has not yet managed to squander. The youth now admits to himself that he has not found happiness nor known how to prolong by much that intoxication with life which he had sought in place of happiness. He wonders: "If my father, after being enraged against me, believes me dead, perhaps in spite of my offense he would rejoice to see me again. What if I return to him very humbly, my head bowed and covered with ashes, and if I kneel before him and say to him, 'Father, I have sinned against heaven and before thee' . . . what shall I do if, raising me with his hand, he says, 'Enter the house, my son. . . ." And already the prodigal is penitently on his way.

From the crest of the hill he sees at last the smoking chimneys of the house. It is almost evening, but he waits for the shadows of night to veil his shabbiness. Now he hears from a distance his father's voice. His knees give way. He staggers and covers his face with his hands, for he is ashamed of his failure. He is famished. All he has in a fold of his tattered cloak is one handful of the sweet acorns which have been his sole nourishment, as they were of the swine he tended. He sees the preparations for the evening meal. He recognizes the figure of his mother who appears on the doorstep. He can hold back no longer, runs down the hill and hastens into the courtyard. He is barked at by his own dog who does not know him. He wants to speak to the servants, but they are suspicious, draw away and go to warn the master. Here he comes!

There is no doubt that he had been expecting the prodigal son, for he recognizes him at once. He goes to him with open arms. The son kneels before him, and, hiding his face with one arm, cries to him, his right hand raised in supplication for forgiveness:

"Father, father! I have sinned gravely against heaven and against you, I am no longer worthy to be called, but at least, like one of your servants, the lowliest among them, allow me to live in a corner of our house."

The father raises him and embraces him. "My son, may the day you returned to me be blessed!" And, joy overflowing his heart, the father weeps. He lifts his head from his son's brow which he has just kissed and turns toward the servants:

"Bring forth the most beautiful robe. Put shoes on his feet, and a precious ring on his finger. Look for the fattest calf in our stables, and kill it. Prepare a joyful feast. For the son whom I thought dead is alive."

And, as the news is already spreading, the father hastens, for he does not want to allow another to say it:

"Mother, the son we wept for is returned to us."

Everyone's joy, rising like a hymn, annoys the elder son. He sits down at the common table only because his father, when inviting him, constrained him to do so. He alone among the many celebrants—for even the least of the servants has been invited—has a scowling face, for he questions why more honor is given to a repentant sinner than to himself, who has never sinned? He is one who prefers order to love. If he consents to be present at the feast, it is only because, acknowledging the fact of his brother's return, he will allow him cheer for only that evening; it is also because his father and mother have promised to rebuke the prodigal tomorrow, and because he himself is preparing to lecture him sternly.

The smoke of the torches rises toward the sky. The meal is over. The servants have cleared the tables. Now, in the darkness, with not a breath of wind rising, the weary household, one by one, retires to sleep. Yet, in a room next to the prodigal's, I know that a boy, his youngest brother, will seek slumber in vain all night long.

THE FATHER'S REPRIMAND

Lord, like a child I kneel before You today, my face wet with tears. If I recollect and render here Your urgent parable, it is because I understand Your prodigal son, it is because in him I see myself, it is because there are times when I hear in myself and repeat in secret the words which, from the depths of his anguish, You have him cry: "How many hirelings of my father have bread in abundance in his house, while I die of hunger!"

And I imagine the father's embrace; in the warmth of such love my heart lifts. I see it all clearly—my own heart beats fast when, at the crest of the hill, the prodigal sees once more

the blue roofs of the house he foresook. What is keeping *me*
then from rushing to *my* home, from entering it? I am expected. Already I see the fatted calf being made ready. . . .
Stop! Do not spread the feast too soon. . . . Prodigal son,
tell me first what the father said to you the day after the festivities of reunion. And Father, though the elder son influenced
you, may I hear *your* voice, at least sometimes, through his
words!

The father speaks: "My son, why did you leave me?"

"Did I really leave you? Are you not everywhere, Father?
I have never ceased to love you."

"Let us not quibble. I had a house that protected you. It
was built for you. Generations labored that your soul might
find shelter there, splendor worthy of it, comfort and purpose.
You, the heir, the son, why did you flee from the house?"

"Because the house imprisoned me. The house is not you,
Father."

"It was I who built it, and for you."

"No, these are not your words, but my elder brother's. You
it was who built the whole world, both the house and what is
not the house. Indeed, the house others built, in your name;
that I know, yes, it was so, others built it than you."

"Man needs a roof over his head. Arrogant boy! Do you
think you can sleep in the open air?"

"Does that take so much arrogance! Poorer men than I
have done so."

"Those are the poor. You are not poor. No one can renounce his wealth. I had made you rich above all men."

"Father, you know that when I left I took with me all
that I could carry of my wealth. What do riches that cannot
be carried away matter to me?"

"All that fortune which you took with you, you spent
rashly."

"I changed your gold into pleasures, your teachings into

imagination, my innocence into poetry, and my abstinence into desires."

"Was it for this that your frugal parents strove to inspire in you so much virtue?"

"For me to burn with a finer flame, perhaps, so that I may be quickened with a new fervor."

"Remember that pure flame which Moses saw on the sacred bush. It burned but did not consume."

"I have known love that consumes."

"The love which I want to teach you refreshes. After a while, what was left to you, prodigal son?"

"The memory of my pleasures."

"And the destitution that follows them."

"In this destitution I felt close to you, Father."

"Then, did it take poverty to send you back to me?"

"I don't know . . . I don't know. . . It was in the aridity of the desert that I loved my thirst best."

"Your poverty made you feel more keenly the worth of riches."

"No, it was not that! Do you not understand me, Father? My heart, so unencumbered, had more room for love. I bought fervor at the price of all my worldly goods."

"Were you happy so far from me?"

"I did not feel far from you."

"Then what made you come back? Tell me."

"I do not know. Perhaps it was indolence."

"Indolence, son? What? It was not love?"

"Father, I have told you, I never loved you more than in the desert. But I became weary from seeking my subsistence each morning. In the house, one eats well at least."

"Yes, my servants see to that. So, what brought you back was hunger."

"Perhaps cowardice as well, and illness. In the end this precarious nourishment weakened me, for I lived on wild fruits, locusts, and honey. Less and less could I endure the discomfort which at the beginning stirred my fervor. At night, when I was cold, I thought how well my bed was made at my father's house. When I was famished, I thought how at my father's house the abundance of the table had always exceeded my hunger. I weakened. I no longer possessed the courage and the strength to resist, and yet . . ."

"So yesterday's fatted calf tasted good to you?"

The prodigal son throws himself sobbing to the ground, his face pressed against the earth. "Father! Father! The wild taste of sweet acorns clings to my tongue in spite of everything. Nothing could make me forget its delight."

"Poor child!" says the father, raising him up, "perhaps I spoke harshly to you. Your brother wanted me to. It is he who makes the law here. It was he who urged me to say to you, 'Outside of the house, there is no salvation for you.' But, it was I who molded you. I therefore know what is in you. I know what urged you forth on your highways and byways. I was waiting for you at the end of your wanderings. Had you but called me . . . I was there."

"Father, could I then have found you without returning?"

"If you felt weak, you did well to return. Go now, go to the room that I have had made ready for you. Enough for today. Rest now. Tomorrow you can speak to your brother."

THE REPRIMAND OF THE ELDER BROTHER

The prodigal tries at first to be condescending. "Older brother," he begins, "we are scarcely alike. No, brother dear, we don't resemble each other at all."

"That's your fault," retorts the elder brother.

"Why mine?"

"Because I am in the right, everything that is in discord with my way is the fruit or seed of arrogance."

"Can I have nothing individual except faults?"

"Don't call good that which leads you away from the right path; you must curb whatever does so."

"It is this mutilation that I fear. What you want me to destroy also comes from the father."

"No, not destroy, I said 'curb.'"

"I understand you quite well. That was exactly how I curbed my virtues. . . ."

"And that is why I now find them in you again. You must now dwell on them. Try to understand me—it is not that you diminish yourself that I propose, but that you elevate yourself. The most conflicting, the most unruly impulses of your flesh and of your spirit must attain harmony, or the worst of yourself must nourish the best, or the best must submit to . . ."

"It was an elevation of self which I sought and found in the desert, and, perhaps, not very different from the one that you propose to me."

"To tell the truth, I should like to impose it on you."

"Our father didn't speak so harshly."

"I know what the father said to you. It was vague. He no longer explains himself very lucidly. One can make him say what one wishes. But I know well what he thinks. I am his sole interpreter, and whoever would understand the father must listen to me."

"I had no trouble understanding him without you."

"It seemed so to you, but you understood badly. There aren't several ways of understanding the father, there aren't several ways of listening to him. And there aren't several ways of loving him, so as to be one with him."

". . . in his house."

"This love brings one back, you must have seen that, since here you are, back. Tell me now, what made you leave?"

"I felt too strongly that the house is not the whole universe. I couldn't help dreaming of other cultures, other lands, and the roads that would take me there, roads still unmarked.

I felt myself to be a new sort of being, striving to reach out.
I escaped."

"Think of what would have happened if, like you, I had
abandoned the father's house. The servants and marauders
would have plundered all our goods."

"That would not have stopped me then, because I had
caught a glimpse of other riches. . . ."

"Which your pride exaggerated for its own reasons.
Brother, impulse is a thing of the past. You will learn, if you
don't yet know, from what chaos man has emerged. He is
not yet quite safe from it. He sinks back with his whole simple-
minded weight as soon as the Spirit no longer lifts him above
it. Don't learn this at a great cost to yourself. The well-
ordered elements in you await only a willigness, only a
weakening on your part to return to anarchy. But what you
will probably never know is how long it has taken man to
shape man. Now that the model has been wrought, let us preserve it. . . . 'Thou shouldst hold fast that which thou hast'
says the Spirit to the Angel of the Church, and it adds,
'That no man take thy crown.' *That which thou hast* is your
crown, it is the sovereignty over others and over yourself.
Your crown—the usurper lies in wait for it, and he is everywhere. He prowls around you, in you. Hold fast, brother! Hold
fast!"

"I had let go long ago. I can no longer control my estate."

"Yes, yes, you can, and I shall help you. I have guarded
your wealth during your absence."

"Look here, there is more to the words of the Spirit, I
know them, I know that you didn't quote all of them."

"Yes, they continue this way: 'Him that overcometh will
I make a pillar in the temple of God and he shall go no more
out.' "

" 'He shall go no more out!' That is what scares me."

"Even if it is for the sake of His happiness?"

"But I have been in this temple. . . ."

"You must have regretted leaving it, since you desired to return."

"I know, I know. Here I am, back. I admit it."

"What good can you seek outside which you don't find here in abundance? Or better, only here is your wealth to be found."

"I know that you've kept riches for me."

"I've kept what you have not squandered, the part which is common to all of us, the land and immovable goods."

"Don't I possess anything else, something of my own?"

"Yes, that special share of gifts that our father may see fit to grant you."

"That is all that interests me. I am willing to possess nothing but that."

"What pride! You will not be consulted about it. Between you and me, that portion is chancy, I advise you not to count on it. It was your share of personal gifts that caused your failure. This personal wealth you squandered at once."

"The other kind I couldn't carry away with me."

"Therefore, you are going to find it intact. But, enough for today. Go inside, into the comfort of the house."

"That I should like, for I am tired."

"Then blessed be your fatigue! Sleep for the present. To-morrow your mother will speak to you."

THE MOTHER

Prodigal son, whose mind still recoils from your brother's words, let your heart speak now. How pleasant it is for you to recline at your mother's feet, with your head on her lap. How sweet it is to feel her caressing hand on your rebellious neck.

"Why did you leave for such a long time?"

You answer only with tears.

"Why weep now, my son? You have been given back to me. I shed all my tears while I waited for you."

"Were you still waiting for me?"

"I never gave up hope. Each night before going to sleep I would think, 'If he returns tonight, will he know how to open the door?' and it took me a long time to fall asleep. Each morning before fully waking, I would think, 'Will it be today that he will return?' Then I prayed. I prayed so much that you had to return."

"Your prayers forced me to return."

"Don't mock me with that smile, my child."

"Oh Mother! I come back to you with great humility. See how I place my forehead lower than your heart. There is not a single thought I had that has not become meaningless now. Here, near you, I can hardly understand why I ever left the house."

"And will you not leave again?"

"I cannot leave again."

"What was it that attracted you outside?"

"I don't want to think about it anymore. Nothing . . . myself."

"Did you expect to be happy away from us?"

"I wasn't looking for happiness."

"What were you looking for?"

"I was looking for myself . . . to know who I was."

"Oh! Son of your parents and brother among your brothers!"

"I wasn't like my brothers. Let's not speak any more about it. I am back now."

"Yes, let us speak about it some more. Don't believe your brothers to be so different from you."

"From now on my only concern is to be like all of you."

"You seem to say this with resignation."

"Nothing is more exhausting than to realize one's difference from others. This journey eventually wore me out."

"You have grown quite old, that is true."

"I have suffered."

"My poor child! Doubtless your bed was not made every evening, nor the table set for all your meals."

"I ate what I could find, and often it was only unripe or spoiled fruit which fed my hunger."

"Did you suffer only from hunger at least?"

"The sun in the middle of the day, the cold wind in the heart of the night, the shifting sand of the desert, the thorns that caused my feet to bleed, none of all that stopped me, but—I didn't tell all that to my brother—I had to serve . . ."

"Why did you conceal that?"

"Evil masters abused my body, exasperated my pride, and gave me scarcely anything to eat. It was then that I thought, 'Why serve for the sake of serving?' And in my dreams I saw the house again. I returned."

The prodigal son again bows his head, and his mother strokes it tenderly.

"What are you going to do now?"

"I've told you: concern myself with being like my elder brother, help manage our goods, like him take a wife. . . ."

"Doubtless you have someone in mind when you say that . . ."

"Oh, it doesn't matter who will be chosen, as long as you choose her. Do as you've done for my brother."

"I should like to choose her to please your heart."

"What does it matter! My heart has chosen. I renounce the willfulness that carried me far from you. Guide my choice. I submit, I tell you. I shall yield my children to you as well. That way my adventure will not seem so futile."

"Listen, there is a child with whom you might already concern yourself."

"What do you mean, and about whom are you speaking?"

"About your younger brother, who was not yet ten years old when you left, whom you scarcely recognized, but who . . ."

"Go on, Mother, what disturbs you now?"

". . . in whom, however, you might have recognized yourself, for he is just like you were when you left."

"Like me?"

"Like you were, I say, not yet, alas, like what you have become."

"Which he will become."

"We must make him become that immediately. Talk to him. He will certainly listen to you, the prodigal. Tell him what disappointments you found on the road. Save him . . ."

"But what causes you such alarm on my brother's account? Perhaps it is simply that likeness of features . . ."

"No, no, the resemblance between you two is deeper. I am worried at present about what should have worried me more at the beginning about you. He reads too much, and doesn't always prefer good books."

"Is it only that?"

"He often perches on the highest tree in the garden from which, you remember, the country can be seen above the walls."

"I remember it. Is that all?"

"He is much less often with us than on the farm."

"And what does he do there?"

"Nothing evil. But it isn't the farmers he visits, it is the ill-bred farmhands who are most different from us that he prefers, and those who are not from these parts. There is one in particular, who comes from far away, who tells him stories."

"Oh, you mean the swineherd."

"Yes. Did you know him? To listen to his tales, your brother follows him each evening into the pigsty. He comes back only for his meal, without appetite, his clothes reeking. Disapproval is futile. He stiffens under restraint. Some mornings at dawn, before any of us are up, he runs off to follow this swineherd as far as the gate when he is leading his herd to pasture."

"He knows that he mustn't go beyond the gate."

"You knew it also! Some day he will leave me, I am sure. One day he will leave."

"No, Mother, I'll speak to him. Don't be alarmed."

"I know that he will listen to a lot from you. Did you see how he watched you the first evening? With what prestige your rags were covered in his eyes! And the purple robe which the father put on you—I feared that in his mind he would confuse the two a little, and what attracted him first of all were the rags. But this thought now appears foolish to me, for, indeed, if you, my son, could have foreseen such poverty, you would not have left us, would you?"

"I no longer know how I could have left you, you, my mother."

"Well, tell him all that."

"I'll tell him all that tomorrow evening. Now, kiss me on the forehead as you did when I was a little child and you watched me doze off. I'm sleepy."

"Go to bed. I am going to pray for all of you."

DIALOGUE WITH THE YOUNGER BROTHER

There is a room next to the prodigal's, fairly large, with bare walls. The prodigal, a lamp in his hand, approaches the bed on which his younger brother is lying. his face turned toward the wall. He speaks in a low voice so as not to wake the child if he is sleeping.

"I'd like to talk to you, brother."

"What's stopping you?"

"I thought you were asleep."

"You don't need to sleep in order to dream."

"Were you dreaming? What about?"

"Do you care? If I can't understand my dreams, I don't think you are the one who can explain them to me."

"Are they that subtle, then? If you told them to me, I'd try."

"Do you choose your dreams? Mine come of themselves, they are freer than I. What for did you come here? Why interfere with my sleep?"

"You aren't sleeping, and I came to talk peacefully with you."

"What could you have to say to me?"

"Nothing, if you start out in that tone."

"Then good-by."

The prodigal goes toward the door and places the lamp on the floor, leaving the room only dimly lighted. Then, returning to his brother, he sits on the edge of the bed and for a long time strokes the boy's averted forehead."

"You answer me more gruffly than I ever did our elder brother. Yet, I, too, rebelled against him."

The restive youngster suddenly sits up. "Tell me, did our brother send you?"

"No, not he but our mother."

"Oh, you wouldn't have come of your own accord."

"But I come as a friend."

Half sitting up on his bed, the boy fixes his gaze on the prodigal. "How could anyone in my family know how to be my friend!"

"You're mistaken about our brother . . ."

"Don't even talk to me about him! I despise him . . . my whole heart is furious against him. It is because of him that I answered you so rudely."

"How come?"

"You wouldn't understand."

"Tell me anyhow."

The prodigal takes his brother in his arms, and the adolescent boy begins to yield.

"The evening you returned I couldn't sleep. All night I kept thinking: I had another brother, and I didn't even know it. That's why my heart beat so hard when I saw you in the courtyard of our house, all covered with glory."

"Alas! I was covered with rags."

"Yes, I saw them, but, just the same, you were glorious. And I saw what our father did—he put a ring on your finger, such a ring as our brother doesn't have. I didn't want to question anyone about you. I knew only that you had returned from very far away and that your gaze at the table . . ."

"Were you at the feast?"

"I know that you didn't see me. During the entire meal you had a faraway look and didn't see anything. I also know that you went to speak to our father the next evening, and that was all right, but on the third . . ."

"Go on."

"If you had said at least a single word of love to me!"

"Did you expect me to come to your room?"

"So much! Do you think I could so hate our brother if you had not talked with him that evening so long. What could you have said to each other? You know very well that if you resemble me, you can't have anything in common with him."

"I had erred gravely against him."

"Is that possible?"

"At least I had wronged our father and our mother. You know that I had fled from the house."

"Yes, I know. It was a long time ago, wasn't it?"

"When I was about your age."

"So that's what you call your wrongdoing?"

"Yes, that was my wrong, that was my sin."

"Did you feel that you were doing wrong when you left?"

"No, I felt within me a sort of obligation to leave."

"What has happened since to change your truth into error?"

"I have suffered."

"And that's what makes you say, 'I was wrong?'"

"No, not exactly. That's what made me think."

"Does that mean that you hadn't thought before you escaped?"

"Yes, I had, but my weak reason let itself be influenced by my desires."

"As later your reason let itself be affected by suffering. So that today you return . . . defeated."

"No, not exactly—resigned."

"But you have renounced being what you wanted to be."

"What my pride induced me to be."

The boy is silent for a moment, then suddenly cries out with a sob, "Brother! I am what you were when you left. Oh, tell me, did you find nothing but disillusion in your wanderings? Is all that I envision outside and which is different from here, is all that only illusion? All the newness I feel in me, is it all madness? Tell me, what was it you met with that was so discouraging? Oh, what made you come back?"

"The freedom I sought, I soon lost. I had to serve as a captive . . ."

"And I am a captive here."

"Yes, but to serve evil masters . . . here you serve your parents."

"But to serve for the sake of serving—doesn't one at least have the freedom to choose his bondage?"

"I hope so. I walked as far as my feet would carry me—like Saul in search of his asses—in search of my desires. But whereas it was a kingdom that awaited him, I found nothing but misery. And yet . . ."

"Didn't you take the wrong road?"

"I walked straight ahead."

"Are you sure? But there are other regions, other lands, without a king, to discover.

"Who told you that?"

"I know it. I feel it. It seems to me that I am already soaring above them."

"What pride!"

"That's something our elder brother must have said to you. And why do you say it to me now? If you had only kept that pride! You wouldn't have returned."

"Then I would not have known you."

"Yes, yes, you would have, out there, where I would have joined you; out there you would have recognized me as your brother. In fact, it seems to me that it is to find you again that I am leaving."

"That you are leaving? . . ."

"Haven't you understood that? Aren't you yourself encouraging me to leave?"

"I would spare you the return, but by sparing you the departure."

"No, no, don't say that to me. That couldn't be what you mean! You also left like a conqueror, didn't you?"

"And that's what made my servitude appear harder to me."

"Then why did you submit to it? Were you already so worn out?"

"No, not yet, but I doubted."

"What do you mean?"

"I doubted everything, including myself. I wanted to stop, to cling to something at last, to the comfort that tempted me . . . yes, I feel it strongly now—I have failed."

The prodigal bowed his head and hid his face in his hands.

"But at first? . . ."

"I had walked a long time across the great wide, wild earth."

"The desert?"

"It wasn't always the desert."

"What did you look for out there?"

"I no longer understand."

"Get up. Look on the table at the head of my bed, there, near that torn book."

"I see a split pomegranate."

"It was the swineherd who brought it to me the other evening, after he had been away for three days."

"Yes, it is a wild pomegranate."

"I know. It is almost unbearably bitter. Yet I know that if I were thirsty enough I would bite into it," says the boy.

"Oh, now I remember—it is that kind of thirst that I sought in the desert."

"A thirst which only this bitter fruit can quench? . . ."

"No, but it makes you love that thirst," answers the prodigal.

"Do you know where to gather this fruit?"

"In a small abandoned orchard which one reaches before evening. There is no wall separating it from the desert. A stream flows there and a few half-ripe fruits hang from the branches."

"What kind of fruit?"

"The same as grow in our garden, but wild. It has been very warm all day . . ."

"Listen," says the young brother, "do you know why I waited for you this evening? I am leaving before the end of the night. Tonight. Tonight, before the sky pales. I have girded my loins. Tonight I have kept on my sandals."

"What! Will you do what I couldn't do?"

"You have opened the path for me, and thinking of you will give me courage."

"On the contrary, it is for me to admire you and for you to forget me. What are you taking with you?"

"You know that as the youngest I have no share in the inheritance. I leave with nothing."

"It is better that way."

The boy asks, "What are you looking at through the casement window?"

"At the garden where our dead forefathers lie."

"Brother . . ." (and the boy who has risen from his bed

now puts his arms around the prodigal's neck, arms which have become as tender as his voice), "come with me."

"Leave me! Leave me! I am staying to console our mother. You will be braver without me. It is time now. The sky is growing pale. Go without making a noise. Embrace me now, little brother; you are taking with you all my hopes. Be strong, forget us, forget me. May you never return. . . . Go down quietly. I am holding the lamp. . . ."

"Come, let me hold your hand as far as the door," says the boy.

"Be careful on the steps . . ." cautions the prodigal.

THE WALL

Jean-Paul Sartre

JEAN-PAUL SARTRE (1905–   ) was offered the Nobel Prize for Literature in 1964. He was the first recipient of the award to refuse it freely, that is without outside pressure, and did so on the basis of his personal attitude toward literary prizes.

Sartre has an international reputation not only as a novelist, playwright, philosopher, and polemist, but also as the founder of the post-World War II literary movement, *existentialism.* His literary works express his existentialist philosophy, which, in turn, determines his moral and political opinions. His writings respond to the questions that the modern man of conscience poses in the face of the atrocities of war, concentration camps, and terrifying nuclear preparedness. Existing in the modern world, says Sartre, requires of man an understanding of the nature of his society, knowledge that he has the freedom of moral *choice,* and recognition of the necessity of personal involvement. First the individual is to make of himself a more human being and then, through social participation, help shape a better world in which he and his fellowmen can realize an ever-fuller humanity. Without denying—and often stressing—the absurdities inherent in human existence, Sartre nevertheless urges the individual to engage himself in the affairs of man.

Sartre himself has fully *involved* himself as a writer—he has been completely *engaged* in the crucial events of his time. The story offered here, "The Wall," published in 1939, has the Spanish Civil War as its background. Beginning in 1936, this was a bloody struggle between the democratic and fascist forces in Spain, a conflict prolonged and rendered more appallingly destructive by the German and Italian intervention on the side of the fascists. One million Spaniards died. The fascists won.

The narrator of the story, in the last hours of his life, before facing the firing squad, *chooses* not to show fear, not to buckle under to the despicable enemy, not to inform on his comrade in order to save his own life—but to remain "clean," to remain a human being to the last. The *absurd,* however, which so often sneaks up to defeat and mock a man's best resolutions . . . does it defeat this man? . . .

THE WALL

They pushed us into a big white room and I began to blink because the light hurt my eyes. Then I saw a table and four men behind the table, civilians, looking over the papers. They had bunched another group of prisoners in the back and we had to cross the whole room to join them. There were several I knew and some others who must have been foreigners. The two in front of me were blond with round skulls; they looked alike. I supposed they were French. The smaller one kept hitching up his pants; nerves.

It lasted about three hours; I was dizzy and my head was empty; but the room was well heated and I found that pleasant enough; for the past twenty-four hours we hadn't stopped shivering. The guards brought the prisoners up to the table, one after the other. The four men asked each one his name and occupation. Most of the time they didn't go any further —or they would simply ask a question here and there: "Did you have anything to do with the sabotage of munitions?" Or "Where were you the morning of the ninth and what were you doing?" They didn't listen to the answers or at least didn't seem to. They were quiet for a moment and then looking away from us began to write. They asked Tom if it were true he was in the International Brigade; Tom couldn't deny it because of the papers they found in his coat. They didn't ask Juan anything but they wrote for a long time after he told them his name.

"My brother José is the anarchist," Juan said. "You know he isn't here any more. I don't belong to any party, I never had anything to do with politics."

They didn't answer. Juan went on, "I haven't done anything. I don't want to pay for somebody else."

His lips trembled. A guard shut him up and took him away. It was my turn.

"Your name is Pablo Ibbieta?"

"Yes."

The man looked at the papers and asked me, "Where's Ramon Gris?"

"I don't know."

"You hid him in your house from the sixth to the nineteenth."

"No."

They wrote for a minute and then the guards took me out. In the corridor Tom and Juan were waiting between two guards. We starting walking. Tom asked one of the guards, "So?"

"So what?" the guard said.

"Was that the cross-examination or the sentence?"

"Sentence," the guard said.

"What are they going to do with us?"

The guard answered dryly, "Sentence will be read in your cell."

As a matter of fact, our cell was one of the hospital cellars. It was terrifically cold there because of the drafts. We shivered all night and it wasn't much better during the day. I had spent the previous five days in a cell in a monastery, a sort of hole in the wall that must have dated from the middle ages—since there were a lot of prisoners and not much room, they locked us up anywhere. I didn't miss the monastery. I hadn't suffered too much from the cold but I was alone; after a long time it gets irritating. In the hospital cellar I had company. Juan hardly ever spoke. He was afraid and he was too young to have anything to say. But Tom was quite a talker and he knew Spanish well.

There was a bench in the cellar and four mats. When they took us back we sat and waited in silence. After a long moment, Tom said, "We're done for."

"I think so too," I said, "but I don't think they'll do anything to the kid."

"They don't have a thing against him," said Tom. "He's the brother of a militiaman and that's all."

I looked at Juan; he didn't seem to hear. Tom went on, "You know what they do in Saragossa? They lay the men down on the road and run over them with trucks. A Moroccan deserter told us that. They said it was to save ammunition."

"It doesn't save gas," I said.

I was annoyed at Tom. He shouldn't have said that.

"Then there's officers walking along the road," he went on, "supervising it all. They stick their hands in their pockets and smoke cigarettes. You think they finish off the guys? Hell no. They let them scream. Sometimes for an hour. The Moroccan said he damned near puked the first time."

"I don't believe they'll do that here," I said. "Unless they're really short on ammunition."

Day was coming in through four air holes and a round opening they had made in the ceiling on the left, and you could see the sky through it. Through this hole, usually closed by a trap, they unloaded coal into the cellar. Just below the hole there was a big pile of coal dust; it had been used to heat the hospital, but since the beginning of the war the

patients were evacuated and the coal stayed there, unused;
sometimes it even got rained on because they had forgotten
to close the trap.

Tom began to shiver. "Good God, I'm cold," he said.
"Here it goes again."

He got up and began to do exercises. At each movement
his shirt opened on his chest, white and hairy. He lay on his
back, raised his legs in the air and bicycled. I saw his big
rump trembling. Tom was husky but he had too much fat. I
thought how rifle bullets or the sharp points of bayonets
would soon be sunk into this mass of tender flesh as in a
lump of butter. It wouldn't have made me feel like that if he'd
been thin.

I wasn't exactly cold, but I couldn't feel my arms and shoulders any more. Sometimes I had the impression I was missing
something and began to look around for my coat and then
suddenly remembered they hadn't given me a coat. It was
rather uncomfortable. They took our clothes and gave them
to their soldiers, leaving us only our shirts and those can-
vas pants that hospital patients wear in the middle of summer. After a while Tom got up and sat next to me, breathing heavily.

"Warmer?"

"Good God, no. But I'm out of wind."

Around eight o'clock in the evening a major came in with
two *falangistas*.* He had a sheet of paper in his hand. He
asked the guard, "What are the names of those three?"

"Steinbock, Ibbieta, and Mirbal," the guard said.

The major put on his eyeglasses and scanned the list:
"Steinbock . . . Steinbock . . . Oh yes. . . . You are sentenced to death. You will be shot tomorrow morning." He
went on looking. "The other two as well."

* *Falangistas:* Members of the Falange, a fascist organization established
in Spain in 1934. It helped to overthrow the republic in the Spanish Civil
War (1936–39), and became the only political party under Franco's regime.

"That's not possible," Juan said. "Not me."

The major looked at him amazed. "What's your name?"

"Juan Mirbal," he said.

"Well, your name is there," said the major. "You're sentenced."

"I didn't do anything," Juan said.

The major shrugged his shoulders and turned to Tom and me.

"You're Basque?"

"Nobody is Basque."

He looked annoyed. "They told me there were three Basques. I'm not going to waste my time running after them. Then naturally you want a priest?"

We didn't answer.

He said, "A Belgian doctor is coming shortly. He is authorized to spend the night with you." He made a military salute and left.

"What did I tell you," Tom said. "We get it."

"Yes," I said, "it's a rotten deal for the kid."

I said that to be decent but I didn't like the kid. His face was too thin and fear and suffering had disfigured it, twisting all his features. Three days before he was a smart sort of kid, not too bad; but now he looked weird and I thought how he'd never be young again, even if they were to let him go. It wouldn't have been too hard to have a little pity for him but pity disgusts me, or rather it horrifies me. He hadn't said anything more but he had turned gray; his face and hands were both gray. He sat down again and stared at the ground, his eyes round. Tom was goodhearted, he wanted to take his arm, but the kid tore himself away violently and made a face.

"Let him alone," I said in a low voice, "you can see he's going to blubber."

Tom obeyed reluctantly; he would have liked to comfort the kid, it would have helped pass the time and he would

have been less tempted to think about himself. But it annoyed me; I'd never thought about death because I never
had any reason to, but now the reason was here and there
was nothing to do but think about it.

Tom began to talk. "So you think you've knocked guys
off, do you?" he asked me. I didn't answer. He began explaining to me that he had knocked off six since the beginning
of August; he didn't admit to himself the situation he was
in and I could tell he didn't *want* to admit it. I hadn't quite
admitted it myself; I wondered if it hurt much—I thought of
bullets, I imagined their burning hail through my body. All
that was beside the real question, but I was calm. We had all
night to comprehend. After a while Tom stopped talking and
I watched him out of the corner of my eye; I saw he too had
turned gray and he looked rotten; I told myself, "Now it
starts." It was almost dark, a dim glow filtered through the
air holes and the pile of coal had made a big stain beneath
the spot of sky; I could already see a star through the hole in
the ceiling; the night would be pure and icy.

The door opened and two guards came in, followed by
a blond man in a tan uniform. He saluted us. "I am the doctor," he said. "I have authorization to help you in these trying
hours."

He had an agreeable and distinguished voice. I said, "What
do you want here?"

"I am at your disposal. I shall do all I can to make your last
moments less difficult."

"What did you come here for? There are others, the hospital's full of them."

"I was sent here," he answered with a vague look. "Ah!
Would you like to smoke?" he added hurriedly. "I have
cigarettes and even cigars."

He offered us English cigarettes and *puros,* but we refused. I looked him in the eye and he seemed irritated. I
said to him, "You aren't here on an errand of mercy. Be-

sides, I know you. I saw you with the fascists in the barracks
yard the day I was arrested."

I was going to continue, but something surprising suddenly happened to me; the presence of this doctor no longer
interested me. Generally when I'm on somebody I don't let
go. But the desire to talk left me completely; I shrugged and
turned my eyes away. A little later I raised my head; he was
watching me curiously. The guards were sitting on a mat.
Pedro, the tall thin one, was twiddling his thumbs, the other
shook his head from time to time to keep from falling asleep.

"Do you want a light?" Pedro suddenly asked the doctor.
The other nodded "Yes." I think he was about as smart as a
log, but he surely wasn't bad. Looking into his cold blue eyes
it seemed to me that his only sin was lack of imagination.
Pedro went out and came back with an oil lamp which he set
on the corner of the bench. It gave a bad light but it was better
than nothing: they had left us in the dark the night before.
For a long time I watched the circle of light the lamp made
on the ceiling. I was fascinated. Then suddenly I started, the
circle of light had disappeared and I felt myself crushed
under an enormous weight. It was not the thought of death,
or fear; it was nameless. My cheeks burned and my head
ached.

I shook myself and looked at my two friends. Tom had
hidden his face in his hands. I could only see the fat, white
nape of his neck. Little Juan was the worst, his mouth was
open and his nostrils trembled. The doctor went to him and
put his hand on his shoulder to comfort him, but the
Belgian's eyes stayed cold. Then I saw the man's hand drop
stealthily along Juan's arm, down to the wrist. Juan paid no
attention. The Belgian took his wrist between three fingers,
distractedly, the same time drawing back a little and turning
his back to me. But I leaned backward and saw him take a
watch from his pocket and look at it for a moment, never
letting go of the wrist. After a minute he let the hand fall inert

and went and leaned his back against the wall, then, as if he suddenly remembered something very important which had to be jotted down on the spot, he took a notebook from his pocket and wrote a few lines. "The louse," I thought angrily. "Just let him come and take my pulse. I'll shove my fist in his rotten face."

He didn't come but I felt him watching me. I raised my head and returned his look. Impersonally, he said to me, "Doesn't it seem cold to you here?" He looked cold, he was blue.

"I'm not cold," I told him.

He never took his hard eyes off me. Suddenly I understood and my hands went to my face; I was drenched in sweat. In this cellar, in the winter cold, in the drafts, I was sweating. I ran my hands through my hair, sticky with perspiration; at the same time I saw my shirt was damp and sticking to my skin. I had been dripping for an hour and hadn't felt it. But that swine of a Belgian hadn't missed a thing; he had seen the drops rolling down my cheeks and thought: this is the manifestation of an almost pathological state of terror; and he had felt normal and proud of being alive because he was cold. I wanted to stand up and smash his face but no sooner had I made the slightest gesture than my rage and shame vanished; I fell back on the bench with indifference.

I satisfied myself by rubbing my neck with my handkerchief because now I felt the sweat dropping from my hair onto my neck and it was unpleasant. I soon gave up rubbing, it was useless; my handkerchief was already soaked and I was still sweating. My buttocks were sweating too and my damp trousers were glued to the bench.

Suddenly Juan spoke. "You're a doctor?"

"Yes," the Belgian said.

"Does it hurt . . . very long?"

"Huh? When . . . ? Oh, no," the Belgian said paternally.

"Not at all. It's over quickly." He acted as though he were calming a cash customer.

"But I . . . they told me . . . sometimes they have to fire twice."

"Sometimes," the Belgian said, nodding. "It may happen that the first volley reaches no vital organs."

"Then they have to reload their rifles and aim all over again?" The boy thought for a moment and then added hoarsely, "That takes time!"

He had a terrible fear of suffering, it was all he thought about; it was his age. I never thought much about it and it wasn't fear of suffering that made me sweat.

I got up and walked to the pile of coal dust. Tom jumped up and threw me a hateful look; I had annoyed him because my shoes squeaked. I wondered if my face looked as frightened as his; I saw he was sweating too. The sky was superb, no light filtered into the dark corner and I had only to raise my head to see the Big Dipper. But it wasn't like it had been; the night before I could see a great piece of sky from my monastery cell and each hour of the day brought me a different memory. Morning, when the sky was a hard, light blue, I thought of beaches on the Atlantic; at noon I saw the sun and I remembered a bar in Seville where I drank *manzanilla* and ate olives and anchovies; afternoons I was in the shade and I thought of the deep shadow which spreads over half a bull ring leaving the other half shimmering in sunlight; it was really hard to see the whole world reflected in the sky like that. But now I could watch the sky as much as I pleased; it no longer evoked anything in me. I liked that better. I came back and sat near Tom. A long moment passed.

Tom began speaking in a low voice. He had to talk, or he wouldn't have been able to recognize himself in his own mind. I thought he was talking to me but he wasn't looking at me. He was undoubtedly afraid to see me as I was, gray

and sweating: we were alike and worse than mirrors of each
other. He watched the Belgian, the living.

"Do you understand?" he said. "I don't understand."

I began to speak in a low voice too. I watched the Belgian.
"Why? What's the matter?"

"Something is going to happen to us that I can't understand."

There was a strange smell about Tom. It seemed to me I
was more sensitive than usual to odors. I grinned. "You'll
understand in a while."

"It isn't clear," he said obstinately. "I want to be brave
but first I have to know . . . Listen, they're going to take us
into the courtyard. Good. They're going to stand up in front
of us. How many?"

"I don't know. Five or eight. Not more."

"All right. There'll be eight. Someone'll holler 'aim!' and
I'll see eight rifles looking at me. I'll think how I'd like to get
inside the wall, I'll push against it with my back . . . with
every ounce of strength I have, but the wall will not yield, like
in a nightmare. I can imagine all that. If you only knew how
well I can imagine it."

"All right, all right!" I said. "I can imagine it too."

"It must hurt like hell. You know, they aim at the eyes
and the mouth to disfigure you," he added mechanically. "I
can feel the wounds already; I've had pains in my head and
in my neck for the past hour. Not real pains. Worse. This is
what I'm going to feel tomorrow morning. And then what?"

I well understood what he meant but I didn't want to act
as if I did. I had pains too, pains in my body like a crowd
of tiny scars. I couldn't get used to it. But I was like him, I
attached no importance to it. "After," I said, "you'll be
pushing up daisies."

He began to talk to himself; he never stopped watching the
Belgian. The Belgian didn't seem to be listening. I knew what
he had come to do; he wasn't interested in what we thought;

he came to watch our bodies, bodies dying in agony while yet alive.

"It's like a nightmare," Tom was saying. "You want to think something, you always have the impression that it's all right, that you're going to understand and then it slips, it escapes you and fades away. I tell myself there will be nothing afterward. But I don't understand what it means. Sometimes I almost can . . . and then it fades away and I start thinking about the pains again, bullets, explosions. I'm a materialist, I swear it to you; I'm not going crazy. But something's the matter. I see my corpse; that's not hard but *I'm* the one who sees it, with *my* eyes. I've got to think . . . think that I won't see anything anymore and the world will go on for the others. We aren't made to think that, Pablo. Believe me! I've already stayed up a whole night waiting for something. But this isn't the same; this will creep up behind us, Pablo, and we won't be able to prepare for it."

"Shut up!" I said. "Do you want me to call a priest?"

He didn't answer. I had already noticed he had the tendency to act like a prophet and call me Pablo, speaking in a toneless voice. I didn't like that; but it seems all the Irish are that way. I had the vague impression he smelled of urine. Fundamentally, I hadn't much sympathy for Tom and I didn't see why, because we were going to die together, I should have any more. It would have been different with some others. With Ramon Gris, for example. But I felt alone between Tom and Juan. I liked that better, anyhow; with Ramon I might have been more deeply moved. But I was terribly hard just then and I wanted to stay hard.

He kept on chewing his words, with something like distraction. He certainly talked to keep himself from thinking. Naturally, I agreed with him, I could have said everything he said: it isn't *natural* to die. And since I was going to die, nothing seemed natural to me, not this pile of coal dust, or the bench, or Pedro's ugly face. Only it didn't please me to think

the same things as Tom. And I knew that, all through the
night, every five minutes, we would keep on thinking things
at the same time. I looked at him sideways and for the first
time he seemed strange to me—he wore death on his face.
My pride was wounded: for the past twenty-four hours I
had lived next to Tom, I had listened to him, I had spoken
to him and I knew we had nothing in common. And now
we looked as much alike as twin brothers, simply because we
were going to die together. Tom took my hand without looking at me.

"Pablo, I wonder . . . I wonder if it's really true that
everything ends."

I took my hand away.

The Belgian approached us. He asked with false solicitude,
"Do you feel ill?"

Tom did not answer.

"I don't know what it is," Tom said ferociously. "But I'm
not afraid. I swear I'm not afraid."

The Belgian did not answer. Tom got up and went to urinate
in a corner. He came back and sat down without a word. The
Belgian was taking notes.

All three of us watched him because he was alive. He had
the motions of a living human being, the cares of a living
human being; he shivered in the cellar the way the living are
supposed to shiver; he had a compliant, well-fed body.
The rest of us hardly felt ours—not in the same way anyhow.
I watched the Belgian, balancing on his legs, master of his
muscles, someone who could think about tomorrow. There
we were, three bloodless shadows; we watched him and we
sucked his life like vampires.

Finally he went over to little Juan. Did he want to feel his
neck for some professional motive or was he obeying an impulse of charity? If he was acting by charity it was the only
time during the whole night.

He caressed Juan's head and neck. The kid let himself be

handled, his eyes never leaving him, then suddenly, he seized
the hand and looked at it strangely. He held the Belgian's
hand between his own two hands and there was nothing
pleasant about them, two gray pincers gripping this fat
and reddish hand. I suspected what was going to happen
and Tom must have suspected it too. But the Belgian didn't
see a thing, he smiled paternally. After a moment the kid
brought the fat red hand to his mouth and tried to bite it.
The Belgian pulled away quickly and stumbled back against
the wall. For a second he looked at us with horror; he must
have suddenly understood that we were not men like him.
I began to laugh and one of the guards jumped up. The other
was asleep, his wide-open eyes were blank.

I felt relaxed and overexcited at the same time. I didn't
want to think any more about what would happen at dawn,
at death. It made no sense. I only found words or emptiness.
But as soon as I tried to think of anything else I saw rifle
barrels pointing at me. Perhaps I lived through my execution
twenty times; once I even thought it was for good—I must
have slept a minute. They were dragging me to the wall and
I was struggling; I was asking for mercy. I woke up with a
start and looked at the Belgian; I was afraid I might have
cried out in my sleep. But he was stroking his mustache, he
hadn't noticed anything. If I had wanted to, I think I could
have slept a while; I had been awake for forty-eight hours.
I was at the end of my rope. But I didn't want to lose two
hours of life; they would come to wake me up at dawn, I
would follow them, stupefied with sleep, and I would croak
without so much as an "Ouch!" I didn't want that, I didn't
want to die like an animal, I wanted to understand. Then I
was afraid of having nightmares. I got up, walked back and
forth, and, to change my train of thought, I began to think
about my past life. A crowd of memories came back to me
pell-mell. There were good ones and bad—or at least I
called them that *before*. There were faces and incidents. I

saw the face of a little *novillero** who was gored in Valencia during the *feria,†* the face of one of my uncles, the
face of Ramon Gris. I remembered my whole life: how I was
out of work for three months in 1926, how I almost starved
to death. I remembered a night I spent on a bench in Granada;
I hadn't eaten for three days. I was angry, I didn't want to die.
That made me smile. How madly I ran after happiness, after
girls, after liberty. Why? I wanted to free Spain, I admired
Pi y Margall, I joined the anarchist movement, I spoke at
public meetings; I took everything as seriously as if I were
immortal.

At that moment I felt that I had my whole life in front of
me and I thought, "It's a damned lie." It was worth nothing
because it was finished. I wondered how I'd been able to walk,
to laugh with the girls—I wouldn't have moved so much as my
little finger if I had only imagined I would die like this.
My life was in front of me, shut, closed, like a bag, and yet
everything inside of it was unfinished. For an instant I tried
to judge it. I wanted to tell myself, this is a beautiful life.
But I couldn't pass judgment on it; it was only a sketch;
I had spent my time counterfeiting eternity, I had understood
nothing. I missed nothing. There were so many things I could
have missed, the taste of *manzanilla* or the baths I took in
summer in a little creek near Cádiz—death had disenchanted
everything.

The Belgian suddenly had a bright idea. "My friends," he
told us, "I will undertake—if the military administration will
allow it—to send a message for you, a souvenir to those who
love you. . . ."

Tom mumbled, "I don't have anybody."

I said nothing. Tom waited an instant then looked at me
with curiosity. "You don't have anything to say to Concha?"
"No."

* *Novillero:* a youngster who is being trained for bullfighting.
† *Feria:* a holiday festival.

I hated this complicity of tenderness. It was my own fault; I had talked about Concha the night before; I should have controlled myself. I was with her for a year. Last night I would have given an arm to see her again for five minutes. That was why I talked about her, it was stronger than I was. Now I had no more desire to see her, I had nothing more to say to her. I would not even have wanted to hold her in my arms; my body filled me with horror because it was gray and sweating—and I wasn't sure that her body didn't fill me with horror. Concha would cry when she found out I was dead, she would have no taste for life for months afterward. But I was still the one who was going to die. I thought of her soft, beautiful eyes. When she looked at me something passed from her to me. But I knew it was over; if she looked at me *now* the look would stay in her eyes, it wouldn't reach me. I was alone.

Tom was alone too but not in the same way. Sitting cross-legged, he had begun to stare at the bench with a sort of smile; he looked amazed. He put out his hand and touched the wood cautiously, as if he were afraid of breaking something, then drew back his hand quickly and shuddered. If I had been Tom I wouldn't have amused myself by touching the bench; this was some more Irish nonsense, but I too found that objects had a funny look—they were more obliterated, less dense than usual. It was enough for me to look at the bench, the lamp, the pile of coal dust, to feel that I was going to die. Naturally I couldn't think clearly about my death but I saw it everywhere, on things, in the way things fell back and kept their distance, discreetly, as people who speak quietly at the bedside of a dying man. It was his death which Tom had just touched on the bench.

In the state I was in, if someone had come and told me I could go home quietly, that they would leave me my life whole, it would have left me cold; several hours or several years of waiting is all the same when you have lost the illu-

sion of being eternal. I clung to nothing. In a way I was calm.
But it was a horrible calm—because of my body; my body, I
saw with its eyes, I heard with its ears, but it was no longer
me; it sweated and trembled by itself and I didn't recognize it
any more. I had to touch it and look at it to find out what was
happening, as if it were the body of someone else. At times
I could still feel it, I felt sinkings, and fallings, as when you're
in a plane taking a nose dive, or I felt my heart beating. But
that didn't reassure me. Everything that came from my body
was all cockeyed. Most of the time it was quiet and I felt no
more than a sort of weight, a filthy presence against me; I had
the impression of being tied to an enormous vermin. Once
I felt my pants and I felt they were damp; I didn't know
whether it was sweat or urine, but I went to urinate on the coal
pile as a precaution.

The Belgian took out his watch, looked at it. He said, "It
is three-thirty."

Bastard! He must have done it on purpose. Tom jumped;
we hadn't noticed time was running out; night surrounded
us like a shapeless, somber mass; I couldn't even remember
that it had begun.

Little Juan began to cry. He wrung his hands, pleaded, "I
don't want to die! I don't want to die!"

He ran across the whole cellar waving his arms in the air
then fell sobbing on one of the mats. Tom watched him with
mournful eyes, without the slightest urge to console him. Because it was useless; the kid made more noise than we did,
but he was less touched; he was like a sick man who defends
himself against his illness by fever. It's much more serious
when there isn't any fever.

He sobbed. I could clearly see he was pitying himself;
he wasn't thinking about death. For one second, one single
second, I wanted to weep myself, to weep with pity for myself.
But the opposite happened: I glanced at the kid, I saw his
thin sobbing shoulders and I felt inhuman—I could pity

neither the others nor myself. I said to myself, "I want to die
cleanly."

Tom had gotten up; he placed himself just under the
round opening and began to watch for daylight. I was determined to die cleanly and I only thought of that. But ever
since the doctor told us the time, I felt time flying, flowing
away drop by drop.

It was still dark when I heard Tom's voice: "Do you hear
them?"

Men were marching in the courtyard.

"Yes."

"What the hell are they doing? They can't shoot in the
dark."

After a while we heard nothing more. I said to Tom, "It's
day."

Pedro got up, yawning, and came to blow out the lamp.
He said to his buddy, "Cold as hell."

The cellar was all gray. We heard shots in the distance.

"It's starting," I told Tom. "They must do it in the court,
in the rear."

Tom asked the doctor for a cigarette. I didn't want one;
I didn't want cigarettes or alcohol. From that moment on
they didn't stop firing.

"Do you realize what's happening?" Tom said.

He wanted to add something but kept quiet, watching the
door. The door opened and a lieutenant came in with four
soldiers. Tom dropped his cigarette.

"Steinbock?"

Tom didn't answer. Pedro pointed him out.

"Juan Mirbal?"

"On the mat."

"Get up," the lieutenant said.

Juan did not move. Two soldiers took him under the arms
and set him on his feet. But he fell as soon as they released
him.

The soldiers hesitated.

"He's not the first sick one," said the lieutenant. "You two carry him; they'll fix it up down there."

He turned to Tom. "Let's go."

Tom went out between two soldiers. The two others followed, carrying the kid by the armpits. He hadn't fainted; his eyes were wide open and tears ran down his cheeks. When I wanted to go out the lieutenant stopped me.

"You Ibbieta?"

"Yes."

"You wait here; they'll come for you later."

They left. The Belgian and the two jailers also left. I was alone. I did not understand what was happening to me but I would have liked it better if they had gotten it over with right away. I heard shots at almost regular intervals; I shook with each one of them. I wanted to scream and tear out my hair. But I gritted my teeth and pushed my hands in my pockets because I wanted to stay clean.

After an hour they came to get me and led me to the first floor, to a small room that smelt of cigars and where the heat was stifling. There were two officers sitting smoking in the armchairs, papers on their knees.

"You're Ibbieta?"

"Yes."

"Where is Ramon Gris?"

"I don't know."

The one questioning me was short and fat. His eyes were hard behind his glasses. He said to me, "Come here."

I went to him. He got up and took my arms, staring at me with a look that should have pushed me into the earth. At the same time he pinched my biceps with all his might. It wasn't to hurt me, it was only a game: he wanted to dominate me. He also thought he had to blow his stinking breath square in my face. We stood for a moment like that, and I almost felt like laughing. It takes a lot to intimidate a man who is

going to die; it didn't work. He pushed me back violently
and sat down again. He said, "It's his life against yours. You
can have yours if you tell us where he is."

These men dolled up with their riding crops and boots
were still going to die. A little later than I, but not too much.
They busied themselves looking for names in their crumpled
papers, they pursued other men to imprison or suppress them;
they had opinions on the future of Spain and on other subjects.
Their little activities seemed shocking and burlesquelike to
me; I couldn't put myself in their place; I thought they were
insane. The little man was still looking at me, whipping his
boots with the riding crop. All his gestures were calculated
to give him the look of a live and ferocious beast.

"So? You understand?"

"I don't know where Gris is," I answered. "I thought he
was in Madrid."

The other officer raised his pale hand indolently. This
indolence was also calculated. I saw through all their little
tricks and I was stupefied to find there were men who amused
themselves that way.

"You have a quarter of an hour to think it over," he said
slowly. "Take him to the laundry, bring him back in fifteen
minutes. If he still refuses he will be executed on the spot."

They knew what they were doing: I had passed the night
in waiting; then they had made me wait an hour in the cellar
while they shot Tom and Juan, and now they were locking
me up in the laundry. They must have prepared their game
the night before. They told themselves that nerves eventually
wear out and they hoped to reduce me to that state.

They were badly mistaken. In the laundry I sat on a stool
because I felt very weak, and I began to think. But not about
their proposition. Of course I knew where Gris was; he was
hiding with his cousins, four kilometers from the city. I also
knew that I would not reveal his hiding place unless they
tortured me (but they didn't seem to be thinking about that).

All that was perfectly regulated, definite and in no way
interested me. Only I would have liked to understand the
reasons for my conduct. I would rather die than inform on
Gris. Why? I didn't like Ramon Gris any more. My friendship for him had died a little while before dawn at the same
time as my love for Concha, at the same time as my desire to
live. Undoubtedly I thought highly of him—he was tough.
But it was not for this reason that I was going to die in his
place; his life had no more value than mine; no life had value.
They were going to slap a man up against a wall and shoot
at him till he died, whether it was I or Gris or somebody else
made no difference. I knew he was more useful than I to the
cause of Spain but I thought at the moment to hell with Spain
and anarchy; nothing was important. Yet I was there, I could
save my skin and betray Gris and I refused to do it. I found
that somehow comic; it was obstinacy. I thought, "I must
be stubborn!" And a droll sort of gaiety spread over me.

They came for me and brought me back to the two officers.
A rat ran out from under my feet and that amused me. I turned
to one of the falangistas and said, "Did you see the rat?"

He didn't answer. He was very sober, he took himself
seriously. I wanted to laugh but I held myself back because
I was afraid that once I got started I wouldn't be able to stop.
The falangista had a mustache. I said to him, "You ought to
shave off your mustache, you idiot." I thought it funny that
he would let the hairs of his living being invade his face. He
kicked me without great conviction and I kept quiet.

"Well," said the fat officer, "have you thought about it?"

I looked at them with curiosity, as insects of a very rare
species. I told them, "I know where he is. He is hidden in the
cemetery. In a vault or in the gravediggers' shack."

It was a farce. I wanted to see them stand up, buckle their
belts, and give orders busily.

They jumped to their feet. "Let's go. Molés, go get fifteen
men from Lieutenant Lopez. You," the fat man said, "I'll let

you off if you're telling the truth, but it'll cost you plenty if you're making monkeys out of us."

They left in a great clatter and I waited calmly under the guard of falangistas. From time to time I smiled, thinking about the spectacle they would make. I felt stunned and malicious. I imagined them lifting up tombstones, opening the doors of the vaults one by one. I imagined this situation to myself as if I had been someone else—this prisoner obstinately playing the hero, these grim falangistas with their mustaches and their men in uniform running among the graves; it was irresistibly funny. After half an hour the little fat man came back alone. I thought he had come to give the orders to execute me. The others must have stayed in the cemetery.

The officer looked at me. He didn't look at all sheepish. "Take him into the big courtyard with the others," he said. "After the military operations a regular court will decide what happens to him."

"Then they're not . . . not going to shoot me? . . ."

"Not now, anyway. What happens afterward is none of my business."

I still didn't understand. I asked, "But why . . . ?"

He shrugged his shoulders without answering, and the soldiers took me away. In the big courtyard there were about a hundred prisoners, women, children, and a few old men. I began walking around the central grassplot, I was stupefied. At noon they let us eat in the mess hall. Two or three people questioned me. I must have known them, but I didn't answer —I didn't even know where I was.

Around evening they pushed about ten new prisoners into the court. I recognized Garcia, the baker. He said, "What damned luck you have! I didn't think I'd see you alive."

"They sentenced me to death," I said, "and then they changed their minds. I don't know why."

"They arrested me at two o'clock," Garcia said.

"Why?" Garcia had nothing to do with politics.

"I don't know," he said. "They arrest everybody who doesn't think the way they do." He lowered his voice. "They got Gris."

I began to tremble. "When?"

"This morning. He messed it up. He left his cousin's on Tuesday because they had an argument. There were plenty of people to hide him but he didn't want to owe anything to anybody. He said, 'I'd go and hide in Ibbieta's place, but they got him, so I'll go hide in the cemetery.'"

"In the cemetery?"

"Yes. What a fool. Of course they went by there this morning, that was sure to happen. They found him in the gravediggers' shack. He shot at them and they got him."

"In the cemetery!"

Everything began to spin and I found myself sitting on the ground—I laughed so hard I cried.

THE
IMMACULATE ARLÉSIENNES

THE
COMPLAINT OF THE BULLS
OF THE CAMARGUE
Frédéric Mistral

FRÉDÉRIC MISTRAL (1830–1914) was a regional poet of great re-
nown. He revived the Provençal language and restored it to great
prestige. He wrote his famous narrative poems in that language,
translating them himself into French. His major work, *Mireille,*
was translated into many languages, including Rumanian, Russian, and Czech. There are four different translations of this poem
into English. Mistral was awarded the Nobel Prize for Literature
in 1904; he shared it with the Spanish dramatist, Echegaray.

As a Provençal folklorist, Mistral gathered numerous regional
folk tales, fables, anecdotes, and popular tales. These were
edited and translated by him and other lovers of the folk literature of that colorful region. The two popular tales which follow
are indigenous to the Midi—the southern part of France.

This genre of tale was intended to give the reader joy, solace,
and to help him pass the time pleasantly. "The Immaculate
Arlésiennes" and "The Complaint of the Bulls of the Carmargue"
are drawn from Mistral's collection of prose sketches in his *Prose
d'Almanach.*

THE IMMACULATE ARLÉSIENNES

The women of Arles are famous, through the length and breadth of the land, not only for their beauty but also for the cleanliness of their persons and their dwellings. There is no other town in France where the homes are as well kept, as clean, as sparkling.

The Arlésienne scrubs and waxes her floors every day, and at least once a week she washes the interior and the exterior of her house with lime. Her bed, table, cupboard, chairs, kneading trough and wardrobe are constantly polished until they look like mirrors. The copper utensils, bed warmers, kettles, caskets and pitchers glisten like gold, and the least iron tool, from the shovel at the fireplace to its grate, sparkle like silver.

It is this, one might say, that does the most honor and is the greatest glory of the women of Arles. And the custom, which passes from mothers to daughters, dates far back. Indeed, it would not be surprising if it actually accounts for the

name of *Arles-le-Blanc* (White Arles) by which the town was
known in the Middle Ages.

And there is a story, true and historical, which reveals to
perfection the pride that the Arlésienne takes in cleanliness.
We found it in a periodical which was published in Arles long
ago, under the joint editorship of Monsieurs L. Martin,
E. Fassin, P. Isac and P. Boschet. The name of the magazine
was *Le Musée* (The Museum).

During a naval battle in which Count d'Estaing surrendered
to the British on the sixteenth of July, 1779, a seaman from
Arles named Pierre Bernat, was killed on the royal ship
Provence.

As you know, in those days it was the parish priest who
kept the records of births and deaths; and, naturally, the notice of the death of Bernat was received by Monsieur Coste,
the priest of the parish in which Bernat had lived. The good
Monsieur Coste registered the death. Then he made it his duty
to personally bring the sad tidings, together with his con-
dolences, to the poor widow—whose name was Marianne
Cabote.

"May the Lord preserve you, my poor Marianne!" the old
priest said to her. "Alas! I have come to report to you a sad
event. . . . It is not wrongly said that

> *The wife of a mariner*
> *Is neither married nor half-married . . .*

But remember that even the good Lord died . . . and those
of us on God's earth and on the sea . . . all of us will some
day join Him . . ."

"Oh! what have you come to tell me?" the woman asked
softly. "Is my husband perchance dead?"

"Yes, Marianne, weep Marianne! For your poor man has
been killed."

"Hush, Father, for God's sake, hush! Don't tell me any
more now . . . You can understand, the blood, the shock,

the terror, the attack . . . Come back in eight days to tell
me the news, don't come back sooner than within eight days
. . . I'd be very much obliged."

The good priest did not understand much of what she had
said, but out of respect for the sorrow of our widow, he left
her, promising to return no sooner than within eight days.

And what did Marianne do? Nimble as a bird, she hastened
to the most skilled scrubwoman in her neighborhood and said
to her:

"Come, my friend, let's go and do a little cleaning at my
house." This said, they immediately began and for the duration of eight days continued, with laughter and song, as if
nothing had happened, to scrub and rub, polish and repolish,
wax and wax again! "Now there, a little more elbow grease.
Here, my dear, let me have a bit more of that fine sand, some
of those soap chips, a little more clay, a drop of that yellow
wax, some of that paint. And do give this another dusting,
and another touch with the whisk broom over there." Done!
—from the sea shell to the drinking mug—from the "coque"
to the "moque," as the saying goes, and from the andirons to
the pot hooks, upon my word, everything was recleaned and
made glossy as a pearl.

"Now," said Marianne to herself, "Monsieur Coste can
come."

The priest came again.

"May our Lord preserve you, my dear Marianne," the good
priest said to her once more, "Alas! I have come to tell you
that your poor husband died. . . ."

Marianne let out a cry that was heard throughout Arles.

"Holy Virgin Mary! My handsome man is dead! What will
I do? What will become of me? Woe is me! Woe is me!"

And her eyes brimming with tears, her hands at her head,
despondent and despairing, she pronounced a hundred *mi-
sericordias* and laments. All the neighbors came to commiser-

ate, all the gossips came running, a crowd gathered in the street in front of Marianne's house.

"Is it possible! My good husband, shall I never see you again! *Aïe, aïe, aïe, aïe!*"

"Poor Marianne!" the neighbors said to each other.

But how about the rest of you, would you believe her to be so aggrieved? Just look at her house—it shines like a cup, you could eat off the floor!

"Isn't she a good housewife? . . ."

"You can say *that* again! A real woman . . ."

"You must give credit where credit is due. Her house is the most immaculate in all of Roquette."

Through her tears and her lamentations Marianne saw and Marianne heard everything. I shall let you imagine for yourselves how delighted she was with the way the other women envied her. An accomplished actress, Marianne cried and mourned on that fateful day, but she also won for herself the glory of being the best housewife in the entire Roquette district of the town of Arles.

THE COMPLAINT OF THE BULLS OF THE CAMARGUE

To Monsieur the Minister of the Interior:

Morituri te salutant (Those about to die salute you)

Your Excellency:

In a bulletin issued on the fourth of September, 1873, you prohibited bull-running and bullfighting, under the pretext that the brutality of such events would accustom the people of Provence to the sight of blood and tend to make cruel the inhabitants of the Midi.

It is always the same story: the people of Provence are brutes, rebels, savages. To hear you talk, one would think that they go about killing their fathers and mothers. But at the same time is it not claimed that the inhabitants of Paris are paragons of virtue? . . .

As this decree concerns us deeply, and as it is apparent from what you stated in it, Monsieur Minister, that madmen and toadies have accused us of horrid crimes, we respectfully but forcefully, as it befits black bulls, protest your assertion.

For we are the bulls of the Camargue, the famous bulls of the seacoast, the celebrated bulls who have never been known to subdue a man wearing a hat, who have wandered through the swamps since the beginning of time, and who have pastured on the dunes by the sea since before Saint Lazar and all the Saint Marys landed in Provence.

We are accused of barbarism, of brutality, of meanness. Ask our herders if we ever gore people who do us no harm; ask all the Mireilles of the Camargue and of the Crau if we do not eat out of their hands the blessed morsels of bread or the *cabridelle* flowers they offer us; ask the horses who graze with us on the salty plain if we ever pick a quarrel with them and whether their white foals do not play peacefully with our black calves.

Now and then one of us saunters away from the herd, nibbles gently on some fatty saltworts, turning his horns in the direction from which the mistral wind blows, or, stretching out like calves under the tamarisks, we are content to gaze at the flowing of the Rhône, occasionally sounding into the distance a doleful bellow.

In the long run, though, such a commonplace life becomes boring. And when our herder realizes that it is melancholy that makes us bellow, he assembles us, with the coming of summer, and says:

"Well, my bulls, how about going to Provence for some running? A bit of ceremonial parading will also cheer you up."

And instantly the strongest and the bravest of us volunteer; we take along a few pretty little cows, and with our own tamer in the lead, we cross the Rhône, happy as the fish in the sea. Raising the dust along the roads, we gallop in the night like a pack of devils. We traverse the Midi towns of Tarascon,

Beaucaire, Barbentane, Bouillargues, Aymargues, Estesargues, Massilargues. Everywhere we come there is a rejoicing: "The Bulls! The Bulls! The Bulls!" they cry, and everybody, the poor and the rich, males and females, runs to meet us, to bid us welcome.

Oh, the splendid *abrivades** at Arles! If you only saw them, Monsieur Minister! Here, at times, four or five hundred men on horseback, with their three-pronged spears and bows on their saddles, come to meet us on the plain, to bring us in. Then, when we arrive with this magnificent escort, we are let loose into the parade grounds, called the *Esplanade de la Lisse.* Ah! what a pretty sight! The bulls, the horsemen, the herders, and the crowd!—what excitement and fervor there is in the air as the thrilled and feverish throng jostles at the guard wall. It is like a tornado, a whirlwind, a madness that is a delight to watch. Everyone is frightened to death but everyone wants to be frightened.

And, Sir, it is that which happens in the arenas that is most beautiful. You probably know, Monsieur Minister, that the arenas of Arles and of Nîmes were built for the running of the bulls. Ah! how we shine in the arenas!

As the poet says:

> *The gate is lifted:*
> *His back covered with maggots,*
> *The beast ferocious*
> *Rushes from his lair*
> *Onto the stage . . .*

A thousand enthusiasts, the fearless ones, the toughest types, the most experienced, surround us at once to snatch off our cockades. But it is not safe for them to as much as touch the streamers of ribbon in our horns!

---

* *Abrivades:* the arrival of the bulls at a gallop, surrounded by men on horseback.

With a shrewd hand
One pulls his tail,
Another slaps the rump
Of the black beast . . .

Now come the Provençal toreadors—Ah! how amusing it
is to have them cavort in front of us, quick as lightning,
goading us with their capes—the Provençal bullfighters' special feat. And when they tackle the three-year-old bulls of the
Camargue, now that is even a finer sight: there they stand,
immobile in the center of the arena, with their flaming eyes
and their horns shaped like crescents; there they stand, alone
against the whole band.

When we feel like playing tricks, then—watch out! Without
warning we rush off in a pack and—good Lord! you ought to
see those so-called brave men of Provence run! Some roll on
the ground out of our way, others flatten themselves against
this or that. They make us double up with laughter.

Yes, it is true that at times, at the height of the fun, someone
is gored; but this is hardly worth mentioning, and the crowd
chants to the accompaniment of the oboe of Nîmes:

If he had stayed home today,
The bull's horn wouldn't have hurt him . . .

On the other hand, when our herders see that we have
become enraged, they drive their spears into our muzzles.
But we merely sneeze, lick the blood, and this revives us like
a pinch of snuff.

But listen to this, do you know what is really ugly? It is the
way they treat us in Tarascon—the Tarasconnais insist on
doing things that way:

They tie heavy ropes to our horns, then they drive us into
the streets, pulling at our heads and lashing us with the ropes
until they overpower us.

On one occasion, Monsieur Minister—and that was truly

magnificent!—the young people of Provence came to see us on the bank of the Vaccarés.

Those were the days of the great *ferrades*—the branding of the bulls, when they used to turn them on their backs and brand the wild young bullocks. An old herder who knew how to read told us that a certain César of Notre Dame wrote thus of this fête held in the year 1600:

"In the Camargue, wild-bull fights are seen almost yearly on the occasion of the branding of the young herds, which customarily the most gallant, the bravest members of the city's highest nobility attend."

So you see, Monsieur Minister, that bullfighting and bull-running are by far not massacres and butcheries but, on the contrary, noble pastimes, male diversions, which those in love welcome as an escape and as a practice that accustoms them to danger.

Nowadays, on Sundays and feast days, the youth, not knowing what to do with themselves, go to smoke and drink absinthe and ruin their bodies in the cafés, taverns, and disreputable places. . . . Then, Monsieur Minister, when you need good soldiers, you have to go look for them among the Arabs! . . .

But let us return to the subject at hand. The law feigns wanting to protect us, but we know better. Once the herders are forbidden to run us, we will witness the arrival of the merciless butchers, who will slaughter us one by one. When a bull happens to gore a man, that is barbarism; when the butchers kill us, that is civilization.

The red bulls of Auvergne—those obese idiots who allow themselves to be fattened up for the kill—considering the sort of creatures they are, it is understandable—they are nothing but cattle. But we, the black bulls, we are not to be cowed. . . . Do not be surprised if some night we, the bulls, bullocks, cows, and heifers plunge into the sea of Provence and swim toward Barcelona or toward Spanish Valencia. We will probably disgrace ourselves in the Gulf of Lion, but, Monsieur Minister, so much the worse for everyone! *Morituri te salutant* (Those about to die salute you).

In behalf of the bovines of the Camargue,

Le Cascarelet.*

* Pseudonym of the author, Frédéric Mistral.

AUTHOR'S BIOGRAPHY

MIRIAM MORTON was born in Russia. Since her adolescence she has lived in this country and, intermittently, in France. She has now devoted a number of years to selecting, editing, and translating outstanding works of Russian and French literature for the young reader. She has been called a "superb" translator by the *Saturday Review,* and other publications have found her translations "beautiful," "masterly," and "remarkable."